All Eyes on Tommy Gunz

PART THREE

Warren Holloway

AMERICA'S NEW STORYTELLER

GOOD 2 GO PUBLISHING

ALL EYES ON GUNZ 3

Written by Warren Holloway

Cover Design: Davida Baldwin – Odd Ball Designs

Typesetter: Mychea

ISBN: 978-1-947340-29-9

Copyright © 2018 Good2Go Publishing

Published 2018 by Good2Go Publishing

7311 W. Glass Lane • Laveen, AZ 85339

www.good2gopublishing.com

https://twitter.com/good2gobooks

G2G@good2gopublishing.com

www.facebook.com/good2gopublishing

www.instagram.com/good2gopublishing

CHAPTER 1

Harrisburg, PA, Dauphin County Prison

THE NEXT DAY, Rakman Hussein was released back into general population after being on administrative lockdown for the last eleven months of his incarceration. All of his movements had been closely monitored, from his mail to his visitations to his phone calls. He was now being moved to the high-security unit C-Block, known for housing drug kingpins, serial killers, and rapists, amongst other high-crime-charged detainees. There was no bail, and he had a federal detainer that was keeping him in custody until trial. So, he did not have much to do other than think about his next move.

Rakman's lawyer fought for him to be able to mix with the general population, since the Feds originally wanted him away from everyone so they would not attempt anything on his life. Rakman decided that instead of trying to mix with the block's chaos, he would sit back and observe to see who he would have taken care of his next move. Being in jail forever was not a part of how his legacy or story was going to end.

Since he was a man of riches and great resources, he would have tried to make a move through his attorney, but the Feds would be expecting him to do just that. So, they monitored his lawyer's finances as well as his calls in and out of prison.

The prison already had strict orders not to release him without having confirmation from the FBI since the Tommy Guns incident down in York County with the fake Federal agents who were eventually traced back to Rakman. The FBI could not understand it. Why would he risk getting someone out that his cousin, Amin Hussein, was trying to kill?

His terrorist roots ran deep and connected him to the IJC (Islamic Jihad Organization), a group of men who conducted terrorist acts around the globe. They would assist him in any decision he made, because he had helped fund them as well as other Islamic radical groups.

One of his associates and diabolical terrorist, Sayyid Azzam, introduced Rakman into this new Islamic way of life. Sayyid was also on the CIA's most-wanted list. So men in his organization were being monitored in order to track him down.

As Rakman moved through the block, he saw a few American-Muslims making salat while others were playing cards, chess, and checkers. Some were getting tattoos in their cells while others were getting high or drinking jailhouse wine. A few others simply stood around to take it all in by observing their surroundings just as he was.

He saw someone who appeared to be really laid back yet aware of his surroundings, so he decided to approach him and start picking his brain a little about his current environment. At the same time, he could maybe recruit him to do a few things he needed done.

As he started approaching the six-foot-two medium-built black guy, the man turned around, alert of his approaching presence.

"Sorry if I alarmed you, my brother. I come in peace," Rakman said, displaying calm and respect. "I noticed you're staying to yourself."

"It's the best way to be around here, so these rats can't say they know you or your case."

"What's your name, if you don't mind my asking?"

"They call me Nino in the streets."

"Yes, I do believe I remember reading about you in the papers when I was in confinement. Anyway, I'm Rakman Hussein," he said while extending his hand to shake.

For the first time, Nino made eye contact with him and

remembered who he was from the local and national news.

"Oh shit! I know who you are from all over the TV. You was trying to blow up my city!" Nino said, looking at him a little more seriously and less welcomingly.

"You can't believe everything you read and see; however, these white Americans are greedy and deserve punishment far greater than I can give them. This country and its leaders are full of corruption."

While Nino listened to him, he tried to figure out Rakman's exact angle. He was not stupid, being as wealthy as he was, so Nino knew his approach did not come without a motive.

Nino was a real smart street nigga who could have been a basketball player. Instead, he came up on the drug game and found the right connection. He was often in the right place at the right time. Being both college smart and street smart added to his business flair. The dark-skinned playboy with curly hair knew his way around money, and he knew how to make it work for him. He also knew people—good and bad people.

Rakman now had his attention as he eyed him up ready to conduct the business for which he had approached him.

"Good brother, do you think you can handle something for me?" Rakman asked, ready to proceed with his next step.

"Before you answer this, I want you to know that what I'm speaking of isn't child's play. However, my brother, I can set you up financially, and even get you the freedom you're in need of right now with the case you have."

Hearing this made Nino's mind go into overdrive processing what he had just said. Not the money; he had his own bread. He wanted to know how this cat was going to get him out of jail. The time he faced was life. Even if he cut a deal, it would be no less than twenty-five years, which in his mind was still life—good time or no good time.

"What can I help you with, Rakman?"

"I have a trial coming up soon, and I need to send out some mail to some of my associates. I cannot do it through my lawyer or in my own name, because it won't make it out. The Feds are watching me close. So there will be a relay of letters. You need to find someone you can trust outside of here that can take care of this once the letters reach them."

"I can do this. But just make sure the data you're giving is 100 percent so there won't be any room for mistakes."

"It is and will be correct. But if you or whoever it is you have helping betray or fail me for some deal with the Feds, I will have you and your entire family killed, even your puppy dog you Americans love so much."

Nino didn't take offense to his response or would-be threats. He was only assuring loyalty; he would have done the same if the shoe was on the other foot. Nino figured he would get his brother, Ali, to take care of business since he was more of the militant type, plus he was Muslim.

"Nino, tonight I'll scribe a detailed letter with instructions to my associates. I'll seal it, and you add the name and address to the person you want it to go to. Make sure you write them a separate letter explaining what they need to do and how serious this is to you and me, because it can be fatal if things go wrong."

"I got this shit! It's as good as done, my man!" Nino promised while walking back to his cell to write the letter to his baby bro and put him up on game.

At the same time, he let him know this was a major play and to keep it under his hat. Nino was all about seeing the free world again, especially going from the good life to the hell hole better known as the Dauphin County Prison.

CHAPTER 2

THREE WEEKS LATER, Candy returned to her place in Atlanta that was clearly bullet-riddled from the shootout with her brother, Fat Money, and the Feds. She stood in the doorway holding her baby boy, embracing him with love, but at the same time feeling alone because the two most important men in her life—her baby bro, Ra Ra, and her baby father, Tommy Guns—were on the run.

Her son was making noise as if he was trying to speak. He sounded cute, not really knowing what was going on.

"It's okay, baby, Daddy and Uncle Ra Ra still love you," Candy said while kissing her son on the cheek.

Candy made her way upstairs to get settled in as much as she possibly could while at the same time seeing how much damage was done to her place. Insurance would cover most of it along with the FBI. The organization had offered funding even though they lost agents, but it was not her fault.

Meanwhile down in Cancun, Mexico, her baby brother, Ra Ra, was sitting poolside at a resort sipping on a frozen piña colada while thinking to himself: "This is the life. I should have come down here sooner!'"

It was his first time in the country. He only knew a little of the language from what he learned in school, yet he was a fast learner when forced to pick it up. His main focus was finding a nice Latina who he could cuff for a little while and pay his way with the rent or whatever, just so he could stay low and out of sight. He didn't want to put anything in his name. The fake ID he was using would only go so far before people started asking real questions.

Having $200,000 in American currency in this country amongst regular Mexicans made him rich. He knew not to flaunt it or he would be dead with his head cut off somewhere. Staying low and blending in with the people was his focus once he exited the resort with one of the two Mexican mamis hanging poolside with him.

While Ra Ra sat back enjoying the poolside view over in Miami, Tommy Guns found his way into the mix of things down in the projects doing what he did best: networking and trying to stay low.

He did find himself a bad-ass chocolate stripper named Kiss, just like a Hershey's Kiss. Her real name was Lisa, but that didn't matter to him. He was all over her, appreciating her luring smile with her pretty white teeth. Her chinky eyes were hazel brown and only added to her exotic look. She had thick thighs, fat-ass perky 36D breasts, and a flat stomach like she hit the gym, but it was just how God had made her.

She definitely was a rida like Keisha in *New Jack City*, which made Tommy Guns gravitate toward her even more, because she stayed strapped to protect all the money she made at the club. Besides, if need be, she would jack a nigga if he wasn't on her time.

Tommy Guns found himself at her crib eating brunch that she made for him with ghetto love and spice. He enjoyed her walking back and forth from the kitchen to the living room while serving his food. Her ass looked sexier each time she walked away in her short shorts, showing off the curves of her ass that were peeking out of her tight-fit jeans shorts.

As he dug into his food, he thought about his kids up north in Pennsylvania as well as his boy in Atlanta. A part of him wanted to reach out to Shari to see his kids, but he knew he had to be cautious.

After he finished the food that she made for him, he walked

into the kitchen as she was cleaning the dishes and straightening up.

"Sexy girl, I have to go take care of some business," he said, coming up behind her and grinding on her soft ass as he kissed her neck and made her feel good. He then took both his hands and cuffed her ass, feeling how soft and sensual it was. "Damn! I love that booty, girl," he said with a smile.

"Don't start something you can't finish, fool!" she said to him as his kisses and caresses stimulated her body.

"Don't worry, sexy girl. I'm going to make you say hello to my little friend when I come back," Tommy Guns said, making her laugh.

"I'll be ready to jump all over you when you come back, too. You want me to have the Hennessy ready? You know I love that Henny Dick," she said with lust in her eyes while licking her lips as if she wanted to take him right then and there.

He kissed her lips once more before he turned and left her to her thoughts of what she wanted to do to him when he returned.

As soon as he exited the crib, he called up the homies from Atlanta. He called up Geez first since he would know where

Little D was.

"My nigga Tommy Guns, what it look like, folk?"

"It's all good where I stand, little nigga," he responded to Geez. "You keeping that paper flowing?" he asked.

"Like a stripper with a fat ass. I got this shit on lock up here, me and the homie."

"Yo, you know where I landed, so you and the homie come down here with ten of them things. The project is doing numbers out here."

"You already know it's paper-chasing time," Geez said, knowing Tommy Guns figured if he could set up shop down there and start a lucrative flow, he would be able to get in with the scene of the Miami bosses like that nigga Turnpike Tito he used to fuck with.

"You think y'all can make it down this way tonight?"

"We ridin'! We'll be there to ball with you, my nigga. Oh, before I forget, I took care of that situation for Fat Money, too. His mom was crying but thankful for it all. You know she seen us all grow up together, so seeing us only reminded her of her son."

"Yeah, I miss that funny fat muthafucka. That's good you

took care of that. Like I said, as long as we breathing, his mom or his kids get what they need, feel me?"

"You ready?"

"See y'all niggas when y'all get here, alright?"

"We hitting them clubs I heard about, too," Geez said before hanging up.

After the call, Tommy Guns went to make a run across the city, before he made his way back to the projects.

As he was walking back to Kiss's crib, gunfire erupted through the air, placing him on alert and making him react by instantly grabbing his .44 Magnum from his waistline. He pulled back the hammer with his thumb and swung the Magnum around toward the direction from which he had heard the gunfire.

It was two young niggas shooting out with each other, so he lowered his gun, uncocked it, and looked on at the two thugged-out niggas banging it out until one of them dropped. The other little nigga ran over to him fast, with the gun still pointing at him.

"Yeah, muthafucka, you come into my hood with that bullshit! Look at you now!" the young buck said while firing off another burst of rounds into the other boy's body, just to make sure he wouldn't get back up.

Tommy became impressed with the young nigga's style.

"This nigga is a G out here in these Miami streets," Tommy Guns said before turning around and walking into the crib to fuck Kiss's sexy ass after he took a few shots of Hennessy with her, which made her pussy even wetter than it already was.

CHAPTER 3

AT 6:03 P.M. in the Dauphin County Prison, Rakman came out of his cell for recreation time to meet up with Nino to see what was going on with him. They met in the middle of the block away from the table and TV.

"My brother, how's it going?" Rakman asked in his strong Saudi accent.

"I got a letter for you, but not out here. Step into my cell so the cameras don't see me passing you anything."

After Rakman followed him into his cell, Nino handed him the letter. He opened it in front of Nino, which allowed him to see it; not that it would matter, because it was in Arabic script. As soon as Rakman finished reading the letter, he gave Nino a look of satisfaction.

"My brother, Allah u Akbar. Your job has been done. You, my friend, will be rewarded just as I said you would. Trust and believe," Rakman said, meaning every word he spoke. He took the letter, tore it up, and flushed it down the toilet. "In a few days, you will be released; however, you cannot mention this to no one, not even those you consider close or loyal. It will sidetrack the plans. Just trust and believe you will have your day of freedom and money."

"Rakman, you have my word that I will not tell a soul about this, because I don't trust anyone with my life at this point," Nino said while thinking about the reality of him getting out.

A part of him wanted to believe it; however, the other part of his mind did not believe it would happen until it happened. So until then, he was going to be quiet and await his turn.

~ ~ ~

At 9:02 p.m. Tommy Guns and his sexy-ass Miami chocolate girl, Kiss, were sitting back after a few rounds of fuck-me-harder and drinking shots of Hennessy in between switching positions. Now they were enjoying watching one of their favorite movies together, *King of New York*, starring Christopher Walken as Frank White, a real fucking boss straight out of jail and taking over. This image was what Tommy Guns had portrayed from day one of his release back in the day. His favorite part of the movie was when Frank shook down the poker game in order to make a statement. Kiss was snuggled up against him and caressing his body with her manicured nails as she, too, enjoyed the movie.

His phone started to ring, which brought a halt to their moment. He glanced over and saw that it was his little niggas from the ATL.

"Damn, Kiss, I got so caught up with you fucking my brains out that I almost forgot I told my niggas to come down here. That's them calling now."

"Answer the phone then, nigga. We had our fun for the night, unless you want some more of this," she said, turning her ass to the side and popping it as he answered the phone.

He couldn't deny how sexy she was or how she turned him on each time.

"What's good, my nigga?"

"Yo, we here OG!" Geez said.

He gave them directions to the spot and then sat up on the edge of the bed ready to get fresh and dressed.

"Yo, Tommy, who the fuck did you give my address to?" she asked while still looking sexy but serious as a muthafucka.

"I just told you, that's my little niggas from ATL. They good, plus I'ma take 'em to strip clubs down here and show 'em how y'all get it done."

"If you stepping out with your boys, then I'm going into

work," she said.

Her work meant the strip club.

"We can jump in the shower together before they get here," he offered.

She got out of bed in the nude and looked flawless. She then walked past him and gave him a salacious licking of her lips with lust in her eyes. She wanted more of him, and without question, he wanted more of her. So he followed her into the shower for another round of quick, explosive sex before washing each other up to get ready for the night ahead.

Once Tommy Guns cleaned up, he made his way downstairs with diamonds everywhere on his wrist in the platinum bracelet, the Breitling watch, and the solo chain with one carat all the way around it.

As soon as he came down the steps, he could hear the roaring of the Hayabusa 1300cc engines from his little homies from ATL. He made his way over to the door, opened it, and noticed them parking side by side.

"Damn! Y'all must have been doing 150 coming down here," Tommy Guns said.

"Yeah, we got up there racing each other and shit. I think

we hit 140 or more," Little D said.

"I gotta get more of them. That would be a nice little toy for a nigga to be in and out of every hood nice and fast," Tommy Guns said. "Yo, come on in, little niggas, so we can handle this BI."

They followed him into the crib. Immediately, Little D and Geez zoomed in on sexy-ass Kiss dressing on point in her Prada top, YSL jeans that fit her every curve, and six-inch red Prada shoes, all flowing with her red lipstick.

"Damn, my nigga, who's the model?" Geez said, trying to be funny.

"This is Kiss, my Miami ride-or-die chick."

"So that's what they looking like down here, huh?" Little D questioned.

"What's up, young bucks. Make sure ya boy here brings y'all by to the club to watch me get to a money bag," Kiss said, swaying her hips visually while luring in the young bucks.

"You could have this bag if my old head wouldn't kill me," Geez joked, which made everybody laugh. Then he handed the bag to Tommy Guns with the money in it. Little D handed him the bag with the ten bricks in it. "Here's three from what you gave me, plus this bag he just gave you is the ten piece you asked about," Geez said.

The money bag contained $380,000.

Tommy opened the bag. He was impressed by his little homies getting to the bread like that.

"Alright, little niggas, we going balls out tonight! We'll hit a few spots and I'll show y'all this Miami life, feel me?" he said while taking two $10,000 stacks out of the bag to put into his pocket. "Wait outside, my niggas. I'll be out in a second," he said.

They stepped out, still having images of Kiss's thick up in them jeans and looking exotic, too.

"Kiss, come here, sexy girl," he said, taking out a five-stack band and giving it to her.

He then kissed her soft lips, which lured him in with her Gucci Guilty perfume for women.

"This is for you and your bills, and for keeping that ass sexy as you do. So get a whole bunch of tight jeans to fit that ass," he said while tapping her backside. She laughed, loving and appreciating his touch. "Take these bags and put them away."

"I'll secure the bags while you go out and play with the

homies. Don't forget to stop by either. If you don't, you won't be getting any of this," she said, popping her ass and then dropping it in those high heels.

There was something about her that made him gravitate toward her each time. Maybe it was the good sex and explosive chemistry accompanied with her exotic look and luring eyes.

Tommy Guns exited the crib. He was all ready to go balling with his homies.

"OG, you know you wrong for still pushing this whip, right?" Little D said after seeing that he still had the stolen 760Li BMW he took from the Spanish crew in York, Pennsylvania.

"I got this, little nigga. It'll be gone soon," he said, knowing he should have gotten rid of it already. "In the meantime, y'all can follow me on them bikes. I'll drive this hot-ass car, little niggas," Tommy Guns said while tripping off his homies.

They followed him club hopping for a minute and living it up to the fullest, one club after another. He even took them to see Kiss do her thing. She went extra hard, making them toss their money in the air at her. Then they made their way to Skyblue nightclub, which was owned by the late Turnpike Tito.

As Tommy was pulling up and parking his stolen whip, he saw the security at the door that he remembered from when he came with Tito. This meant someone in Tito's family was still running the business and keeping his name alive.

Tommy also recognized the new custom sky-blue F-430 Ferrari with white leather interior parked directly in front of the club. It looked just like one of Turnpike Tito's whips.

Little D and Geez were right behind Tommy Guns securing all the compartments of the bike. They then followed behind their old head to the club.

"This spot looks real official, OG," Little D said.

"There's a lot of Miami elite up in here, y'all. People that know people and bosses that know cartel niggas, you feel me?" Tommy said while walking up the steps with his ATL homies. "They with me," he said as he handed the security a $100 bill.

"Good to see you, Tommy Guns," the bouncer said. He added, "If you need anything special tonight, I can call it in for you."

"I'm good. I appreciate you though," Tommy said upon entering the club that was blasting DJ Khalid's new shit.

The club was going hard as he was living the boss life.

Once inside, he secured the VIP suite overlooking the dance floor. Each one of them looked the part of a young boss and baller.

Tommy scanned the floor, checking out all of the women. He saw that they all came out wearing their best, from one name brand to another. What caught his attention down in the mix of the crowd was a Spanish nigga who looked just like Turnpike Tito.

The same person he was looking at stopped to speak to one of the bouncers. The bouncer then turned around and pointed toward the suite in which Tommy Guns and his little homies were. Tommy didn't know what to think at first, but then it came to him. This nigga might know Turnpike Tito.

The suite entrance opened as two six-foot-six bodyguards walked in, followed by the man Tommy saw on the floor.

"What y'all niggas want?" Geez asked with a bottle of Moët in his hand.

He was ready to crick one of the big niggas in the head, plus he snuck his strap in, in case anything went down.

"Someone wants to speak with your boy Tommy Guns over there."

As the words flowed from his mouth, the Latino-looking Turnpike Tito parted through them. He stood six foot even and weighed 190 pounds. With his slicked-back black hair, he looked like a Miami boss, with diamonds flowing over his watch bezel, pinky tiny with a matching bracelet. The sky-blue linen two-piece with the white gator belt and shoes set his look off even more, making him look not only like a boss but like money.

Little D, Geez, and Tommy Guns all watched this nigga close as he approached.

"I'm Tony El Fantasma—the Ghost. I like to move without being seen, but that's another topic. You had dealings with my little brother, or as you knew him, Turnpike Tito, correct?"

"Yeah, he was good people."

"The remainder of your tab to him belongs to me, because it was, or should I say is, my money," Tony said real calmly yet with power.

Tony was known in the underworld to those of his stature as being a violent and vicious killer. He earned his power through blood, bullets, and plenty of cocaine distribution. His suave yet up-front business skills allowed him to get involved with those around the world connected to power and influence, making him an even stronger force to reckon with.

"See, amigo, I know that you've been running for your life and freedom, so I didn't find a need to chase behind you. However, now we're face to face in my city. We need to resolve this financial situation we have," Tony said, referring to the $650,000 he was owed.

Tommy stared into his eyes and saw the truth, and he knew he was definitely about his paper. At the same time, he thought about how he could get back into get this money while on the run, since he just had his little homies bring ten blocks through, but that wouldn't last long.

"Tony, with me running, I left a lot of my money up north in stash houses. No matter what, it's safe. I did make moves in ATL with my little homies here. I can get you $200,000 in the morning, and the rest in a week or sooner," Tommy promised, trying to keep it real with the suave goon.

He had no idea if any of his men in the club were shooters. Men like him in power did not go too far without a team ready to put shit down.

"How do know I can trust you to leave here tonight and

meet me in the morning with the $200,000?"

"Because I'm the realest nigga you'll ever meet, plus I fucks with your brother, Tito, like that. I wasn't about to play with his bread, so what makes you think I'm going to do that to you and y'all's family? After I pay you in full, I want to continue the family business, if it's not a problem with you?"

Before Tony responded, he leaned in and whispered to his goons. Once he spoke to them, he let Tommy know what he was thinking.

"I like you, amigo, and your confidence and how you carry yourself. I know my brother wouldn't have dealt with you otherwise. I'll see you tomorrow at the ports. I have property over there. You won't miss me or my men. Be there at 12:00 noon. Don't be late or waste my time."

"I'll be   there because time is money."

Tony exited with his team of security. Little D and Geez were ready to ride, not seeing the bigger picture of what Tommy Guns was putting together.

"What up, my nigga? We can smoke that fake-ass Tony Montana muthafucka!" Little D said, all hyped and feeling the buzz from the Moët.

25

"Calm down, my nigga; we needed this to happen. I'm going to keep my word. I hope he keeps his. I do know that if this plays out the way I want it to, we all going to eat and lock down the East Coast with bird play."

"I'm about that life! I can see me now, state to state and city to city, fucking bitches and counting money!" Geez said as they all gulped back their bottles of champagne and thought about their next power move.

CHAPTER 4

AT 11:00 A.M. the next morning in Harrisburg, Tommy Guns's baby momma, Shari, walked outside to check her mailbox. As she reached inside, she noticed the unmarked FBI car with two agents inside laying on her house with hopes of taking down Tommy Guns. She waved at them and allowed them to know that she saw them as much as they saw her.

"Assholes!" she said aloud, still smiling and waving at them before going back into the house and taking a seat at the dining room table to go through the mail.

She came across a postcard and flipped it over to read the small print, date, and time. There was a picture of a hotel and resort by the beach on the front. A smile formed on her face and she flashed back to when she and Tommy went to the same resort years ago. He was now sending her a message to meet him there, but first she would have to figure out how to get rid of the Feds following her.

Shari got her sons ready for the day as she normally did, before dropping them off and then working second shift as a CNA at the Harrisburg Hospital. Unbeknown to the FBI, she already put in for time off, not knowing Tommy would send for her. She simply wanted to spend time with her kids since it was the end of the school year. She wanted to treat them for their good grades and for making it to the next grade.

She also secured the $300,000 that he requested in the fine print on the back of the postcard. Once she got herself and the kids together, she made her way uptown in her black Honda Accord.

She pulled over at Tommy's mom's house like she normally did and dropped off the kids while she went to work. They made it into the house as the Feds watched her go inside as usual.

"Grandmom!" little Tommy said with excitement as he rushed over to her.

She embraced him with a grandmother's love and kisses.

"Somebody is having a birthday soon!" Mrs. Anderson said to her grandkids.

"It's me, Grandmom. I want a fast car like my dad!" little Tommy said, full of life and innocence.

"Grandmom, what'd you cook today?" Tyrese asked, always hungry for her cooking.

"I made seafood salad with shrimp, fresh crab meat, and lobster with all my love," she said, smiling at her grandbaby. "Shari, are those FBI people still following you around?"

"Yes, ma'am. They parked across from your house. They stupid like I don't know they're following me everywhere. Even when I go to work, they'll have one in the car and the other in and out of the hospital checking up on me."

"They get on my last nerve sitting out there like they ain't got nothing else better to do."

"Well, I'm going to send for an Uber. I'll see you later. Come on, boys."

"Mom, I want to take some of Grandmom's seafood salad," Tyrese begged.

She gave him a look which meant she was in a hurry. Mrs. Anderson caught the look, so she jumped in.

"I'll make him a bowl he can take with him," she said while hurrying to make a bowl.

Then they made their way out through the back door over to the Mini Mart on 2nd and Maclay Streets, where the Uber driver picked them up and took them to the airport. Shari put her head back as the driver took off. Now without the Feds following her, she could see the man she cared about so much. While at the same time, the kids could see their father.

They did not know in advance where they were going because she wanted it to be a surprise that they would appreciate. She was also having thoughts of being intimate with him, since it had been so long since she allowed anyone into her life since Tommy Guns went on the run for his life. She had been more consumed with taking care of her children and had not allowed anyone into her life or space with all that had been going on. She had been focused on moving up to an LPN or RN by taking classes in between work. She wanted more for herself and her kids.

CHAPTER 5

IT WAS 11:59 A.M. in Miami when Tommy Guns, Little D, and Geez pulled into where Tony's import/export company was located. Tommy still pushed the stolen BMW with Tony's men following behind him in two separate H2 Hummers. It was Tony's way of keeping an eye on them while at the same time keeping Tommy Guns honest. His men followed them from the club last night, tailing them all the way until this morning. Tommy Guns saw that they were being followed and realized the power that Tony had compared to his brother.

Tony was already there at the ports with his team of loyal assassins. Tommy saw the sky-blue Bentley Flying Spur parked between two all-white G55 Mercedes Benz trucks with dark tinted windows.

Tommy Guns now got the impact of who he was dealing with. He definitely would have to get this nigga's paper, or the Feds would be the least of his worries.

As soon as the BMW came to a stop, all of Tony's men in the Benz trucks exited. They were strapped with MAC-11s fully loaded with thirty-two in a clip and one in the chamber.

Four men from each truck made their presence clearly felt as Tommy and his little homies started making their way over to the car. At the same time, the men in the two H2 Hummers also stepped out, leaving Tommy Guns and his crew blocked in, but mostly to protect Tony.

As they walked up, one of Tony's men opened the back passenger side of the Bentley. Tony exited with a supermodel-looking Latina with long, silky brown hair and curves flowing over the fabric of her clothing. She had long legs and glowing green eyes that sparkled under the noon Miami sun. She was a really sexy Columbian and looked like Paola from the *90 Day Fiancé* television show. She wasn't there to look good; however, that may be a distraction to most. But Tommy saw her caressing Tony's arm with one hand while the other hand was holding a gold-plated .45 automatic with a white pearl handle and gold-rigged silencer just in case shit went wrong.

Tommy wanted to get straight down to business, so he extended the bag of money to Tony; but Tony didn't take it, as if he was too good or too powerful. Instead, he nodded to one of his goons and they secured the bag.

"There are three hundred stacks in there. That's one

hundred more than I said yesterday. It's my way of showing you how serious I am about continuing doing business with you," Tommy said, adding the extra money to influence Tony's decision to want to do business with him.

He took the money that Geez and Little D brought down last night.

"I see you're a man of your word and potentially great worth. If you choose to continue doing business, clear what you owe and we'll go from there. I know *mi hermano* saw something in you that made him trust you as he did."

"He saw the hunger in my eyes; besides, I'm a real muthafucka who knows how to get to a dollar."

Tony smirked just as the beautiful Latina on his side did.

"Well, amigo, call me when you're ready with my money, and then we'll talk about the future of you rebuilding this empire."

"I won't let you down. Another thing, I see you're still keeping your brother's legacy alive with the sky-blue theme."

"Of course, the sky is the limit," he said, turning with the sexy Latina and getting back into his car.

His goons followed him and got into the trucks. They took

off as the Bentley Flying Spur merged in between the two Benz trucks.

"What up, OG, Tommy?" Geez said.

"We about to get to it on another level. This nigga connected for real, plus his team is on point!" Tommy Guns said.

"That Spanish bitch is on point. I need something like that on my side strapped up like she was," Little D said.

"Yeah, she's a good distraction that would kill ya enemies in a heartbeat," Tommy Guns said. "Let's get the fuck outta here so we can figure out this money shit to get them bricks from this nigga Tony. What you call him last night, Little D? A fake-ass Tony Montana, nigga?"

"He's the real deal now from what I'm seeing. He's about that life. I can't hate on him now!" Little D admitted while getting on his motorcycle and revving it up.

He raced behind Tommy and passed him as he and Geez headed back up to Atlanta to secure more money for the new line of cocaine they were about to get into with Tony the Ghost.

~ ~ ~

At 3:03 p.m., Tommy Guns and his Miami sweetheart,

Kiss, were sitting on the couch watching videos on BET and checking out the rappers fronting like they really lived the life that he woke up to every day. He thought the shit was funny how they talked about cars and money. They didn't have to sell records in order to get the money they always talked about. A real-life scam in the rap game was taking the MC out of rapping and what it used to be.

As he sat enjoying the videos and his thoughts on them, gunfire outside of the crib erupted, which got his attention because it was so close. It was certainly not off in the distance as it was sometimes throughout the day.

When he opened the door, he saw that it was the same young nigga who was shooting out the other day. But this time he was strapped with a 9mm Uzi with a fifty-clip magazine. He was spraying heavily until the other little nigga ran off. Tommy Guns saw the young buck holding his ground, so he walked over to him to get at him about his swag, of which he took notice.

"Yo, what's good with you, young buck?"

"Ain't shit! Them fools trying to get money on my ground. I can't let them fools do that! Then they'll move me out the more they move in. So, I hold it down out here."

Tommy laughed, appreciating the young nigga's thoroughness.

"So, you get to that paper out here, huh?"

"That's what I do, folk. I live for this shit," he said while gripping the Uzi.

"What you moving? Powder, weed, ex, molly?"

The little nigga looked on at Tommy Guns and wondered why the fuck he was asking so many questions. Then he took a moment and saw his face and flashed back to the nationwide news and social media posts about this nigga being FBI's most wanted and a stone-cold killer himself as the media painted the picture.

"I got that shit that made Scarface feel numb to the world," he said. "I'm trying to move enough to get a whip like yours, folk. That 760 BMWLi is boss shit. Plus, it looks fast as a muthafucka."

"Yeah, it's alright. What they call you out here, little homie?"

"Tre Da Hard Way. Tre for short. I'm about that life with this getting money and taking out niggas in my way, feel me?"

"I hear ya, my nigga."

Tre was sixteen years old. He stood five foot seven and only weighed 150 pounds, but he was full of life and ready to get to a dollar. Tre's braids were freshly done and flowed with his dark skin and baby face. He stood there wearing a white tank top; Evisu shorts; black, red, and white Jordan IIIs; a black G-shock watch; and a black diamond chain with his nickname, Tre, on it.

"So, what you working with, Tre?"

"I take a half a bird and then break it down to dimes and twenties. I sell them in bundles to the homies around here. The other half I sell eight balls and shit to move the work fast."

"I see you got a good thing going right here."

"I did until my connect got laid out in a robbery last week, so I got to find a new line."

"I guess my timing is a muthafucka. I'ma put you in position to get you one of these BMWs and more."

"Yo, when I'm done with my work, I'll get at ya fo' sho'!"

"You already know who I am, so I don't need to introduce myself; and from my hood to yo' hood, I'm still the realest nigga. You know where to find me, young nigga," Tommy said before turning around and walking back to Kiss's crib.

"I respect you, gangsta OG. You all on the news how they said you put that undercover Fed down. That was some real shit," Tre said.

Tommy nodded his head as he walked to the crib, ready to plug the young buck in to make money and expand. His only worries were staying out long enough to build an empire that would exceed him yet take care of everybody in his family and on his team.

CHAPTER 6

TOMMY WAS AT the Miami Hilton and Resort at 7:02 p.m. when Shari came into the lobby. He was in the tuck to see if she had been followed like the shit that had happened in Baltimore. Once he saw that she was alone with the kids, he made his way over to her. He was wearing a baseball cap pulled down over his head to cover his face and was also assisted a little by the shades he was wearing.

"What's up, sexy lady?" he said, getting her attention.

She turned and looked at him. She was ready to check him for flirting with her, until he briefly took off the glasses and hat, which allowed her to see who he was. She lit up smiling inside and out. The kids were even happier.

"Daddy, Daddy! I love you and I miss you so much!" little Tommy yelled.

"I love you, too, Dad. I wish you could come around more!" Tyrese said while hugging his father.

"I'm here now, and we're going to have some fun family time, alright?" he said, becoming a family man and a loving father, which was worlds away from the violence the FBI knew him to impose on those in his way.

Shari found her way into his embrace, smelling him and missing his Sean Jeans Unforgivable fragrance.

"I miss you just as much as the kids do," she said, kissing his lips and reminding herself and him what it was like to be with one another.

"Let's go up to the suite I got us. We're going to have a big day tomorrow for the birthday boy," he said, making sure his son knew that he didn't forget.

They made it up to the room and planned their next day, in between running around the suite and having fun being in each other's presence. They all watched movies, ordered room service, and spent quality family time together.

The kids were tucked away asleep at 10:04 p.m. They could now have some alone time to be intimate as well as talk about the important things in their lives.

"I brought that money down you asked me to get to," Shari said, pointing to her bags. "It's in my Gucci bag."

"I'll get it later. I want to talk to you about something serious. I want to know if you would leave the country with me."

"Are you serious?" she asked, all ready to go wherever her man asked because of the love she had for him.

At the same time, she thought of the reality of the question and having to uproot the kids from school to take them to another country that would be foreign to them.

"Yeah, I'm serious."

"I would do anything for you, Tommy, and you know this, but we have to think about the kids. What about them?"

"Okay, what if I leave the country and then send for you and them?"

She leaned in to kiss him with love and understanding of what he was thinking and going through.

"I love you. I wish that you'll always be safe. Just know I'll come wherever you are and whenever you want me to. I'm ya ride-or-die chick from high school," she said, getting a smile out of him when he thought about how they had met.

Her lips found his once more. This time her hands roamed his body and turned him on. At the same time, they undressed each other, with their clothes falling to the floor. He climbed on top of her and kissed her neck with passion. She stroked his erect dick with her hand, wanting it all in her tight body that had been deprived for over a year.

"Be nice, okay? I haven't had it in awhile," she let out in a low sexual tone as she guided his long, thick stiffness into her warm, tight, wet body.

"Mmmmmh!" she let out, embracing the feeling as he thrust into her tightness. "Mmmmmmh, mmmmmmh, mmmmmmmmh." Her moans picked up the more the sensation of pleasure streamed through her body. The sweet sweat of their bodies in the air stimulated their mood as he took each stroke deeper and deeper.

"Aaaaaah, Tommy! Tommy, mmmmmmmmh, mmmmmmh!"

Her moans became intense as the orgasmic sensation was stirring in her body, only making her wetter, hornier, and even more heated as the buildup of the pulsating feeling took over her body. She could feel herself about to cum with each stroke as he was going in and out, in and out, side to side, and deeper and harder.

Her body was reaching its peak. Not having had sex for over a year made her orgasmic fire yearn to erupt from her body. She could not hold it back as her moans flowed from her mouth.

"Ohhhh, Tommy! Ohhhh! Oh God! Mmmmmmmh, mm-mmmmmh, aaaah, aaah, aaaaaah, aaaaah!"

The wave of surging sensation streamed through her body with every deep thrust of his hard, stiff thickness, making her body feel so much sensation. She squirted her love juices that she could no longer contain inside of her. Her moans were music to his ears as he picked up his pace, going faster and faster, deeper and deeper, and harder and harder. The action made him reach the peak as he bust inside her as his body tensed up with each stroke that released the wave of pleasure. With her lips to his neck, she embraced the orgasm she was feeling taking over her. Her heart and mind loved it all as memories of the good days came to her mind.

"Mmmmh! Damn, you feel so good, Tommy. I really miss you, but I miss this dick, too."

"I can't lie, Shari, you still got that good-good!" he said, still slow-stroking her soaking wet and warm pussy, wishing he could do this all day and night.

Her lips now kissed on his body. She wanted more orgasms before the night was over.

"You want to give it to me from the back like you used to?"

she said while kissing his body and at the same time making her pussy squeeze his dick as she worked her hips in motion to get all of him.

"Yeah, turn that fat ass over and I'ma do what I do. Make that ass clap!" he said, making her laugh as she looked over her shoulder back at him as he entered into her, slamming hard and making her ass clap against his flesh.

"Give it to me! Mmmmmmh, mmmmmmh! Yes, right there, baby, mmmmmh!" she moaned as she felt the wave of pulsating sensation take over her body. At the same time, she backed her ass into his long, hard dick. "Aaaaah, aaaah, aaaah! Give it to me!" Shari yelled out as she let her inner sexual animal want more of his dick in every way, not knowing when she would get it again.

"I'm cumming! Mmmmh, ooh God! Mmmmmmh, right there! Mmmmmmmhh!"

Her body could not stop cumming over and over. He, too, could feel himself cumming with each deep thrusting motion into her wet pussy.

"Aaaaaah, yes! Aaaah, aaaaah, aaah!"

"I like this wet pussy! Damn, you feel good!" he said while

44

thrusting hard into her wet love spot before busting deep inside of her.

His motion came to a slow halt before he pulled out and lay on his back beside her while laughing.

"The kids are sound asleep in the other room. Remember when they ran in on us as we were in deep lovemaking? All our moaning and shit had woken them up, and Tyrese and little Tommy were asking you about what I was doing to you," Tommy Guns said, reflecting back to a few years ago when life together as a family was memorable.

"That was funny. My poor babies were scared," she said while thinking back to that night. "They know better now."

She turned toward him and caressed his chest as they continued to talk about life now and the life they used to have together. Without question, Shari would ride for him, and he knew this. But he would need to get all the pieces in play with getting money, connecting with Tony, and rebuilding an empire in which he could make money while he was in another country.

CHAPTER 7

AT 7:00 A.M. the next morning in Harrisburg, the FBI agents were now aware that Shari had managed to slip past them. And to make matters worse, she did it with two agents tailing her. When Agent Johnson was made aware of what had taken place, he became enraged at his agents for losing this woman and her children.

"How the hell did you men allow this woman and her two kids to disappear from your sights? Now no one can tell me where the hell she is! Without a doubt, she is with the one person we're trying to take down!"

"Sir, we sat on the house and her car all night until we decided to knock on the door looking for her. The owner of the house, Mrs. Anderson, claims she was sleeping when Shari left. She didn't know her car was still in front of her house," the agent tailing her admitted.

"I want men searching all of her known hangouts, her workplace, and people she associates with there. Maybe they'll know where she is!"

As Agent Johnson continued speaking, his phone rang and

got his attention. He picked up on the second ring, pausing his speech to his men.

"Agent Johnson here."

"Johnson, Jack Ross here. I got some information leading to where one of our suspected fugitives is. I already connected with the FBI office close to our fugitive. They'll go ahead and secure him and then get back to us with the updates."

"Sounds great, sir. I'll be on standby waiting on your call," he said, hanging up the phone and focusing back on addressing his men.

~ ~ ~

By 8:00 a.m. in Cancun, Mexico, Ra Ra was lying in bed asleep with his Mexicanas who he had sex with the night before. Each one of them looked like exotic models and strippers. Each one appreciated their American balla who showed them a lot of love and money last night. He treated them like queens in every way, and their bodies embraced his and one another's.

Ra Ra was living the life in Mexico: enjoying the food, the women, the view, and the position of being a young boss.

By 8:01 a.m. the FBI was now fully alerted to the fugitive's position, so they were ready to move in to secure him and finally take him down.

~ ~ ~

By 8:15 a.m., Tommy Guns, Shari, and the kids were getting ready to go to the park in Miami for the day. They were all in the elevator making their way down to the first floor. The kids were full of excitement and ready to have fun and get on roller coasters. The elevator chimed as they stopped on the first floor. They headed toward the exit ready to leave for the day.

~ ~ ~

At 8:16 a.m., in Mexico, Ra Ra was awakened by a slamming door in the hotel hallway. At the same time, he became paranoid knowing he was on the run and the Feds would be looking for him. He jumped up from the bed with his heart pounding as he made his way over to the door. He knew the warrant for him was dead or alive, and he was not about to go out like that without killing a few Feds in the process. He looked back at the sexy-ass Mexicanas and thought about last night and how he would miss that good life if he got caught.

~ ~ ~

By 8:17 a.m., Tommy and his family had made their way

to the hotel exit. He instantly saw Miami-Dade parked by his stolen 760Li. Being paranoid and thinking that they were onto him, his hood instincts kicked in. He turned back around and made his way up to the receptionist desk, where a good-looking, golden-tanned blonde greeted him with a smile.

"Excuse me, I would like to use the hotel's limo service to take my family out today if that's possible," he asked, placing two $100 bills on the counter to avoid her attempting to give him an excuse about them being booked or too busy.

"Thank you kindly, sir. Your car will be out front in just a second," she informed him after running her fingers across the keyboard to see if a driver was available.

She then picked up the phone and called the driver waiting out front. Tommy and his family stepped inside. The kids were happy and ready to go have some fun, while Shari felt good about last night's good sex and today's family time.

As the limo drove past the 760Li BMW, Tommy could see the cop in his squad car with a blonde-haired chick's head going up and down on him and sucking him off. Tommy started laughing because his paranoia made him think shit was about to hit the fan.

"What's so funny?" Shari asked.

"The cop in the car beside my BMW was getting head, and I thought he was onto me," he told her.

She found it funny as she looked back to see what he was looking at.

~ ~ ~

The FBI was filling the halls of the Cancun resort at 9:00 a.m. looking for Ray Smith a.k.a. Ra Ra. Ra Ra could now hear the commotion in the hallway, which made him curious to know what was going on out there.

In that same split second, the Feds stormed the hotel room to which they had a key card. Their guns were aimed and ready to take him down. The man in the bed quickly jumped up and thought that he was being robbed as he put his hands up and had his eyes wide open. He was scared to die or be robbed. The agents immediately realized this fifty-year-old white male was not the Ray Smith for whom they were looking.

Ra Ra was ten rooms down the hall looking out of his suite. He wanted to know what the noise and yelling were all about. Right then, his heart and mind started racing fast upon seeing the Feds in tackle gear come out of the suite down the hall. He quickly shut the door and ran back over to the bed to gather his things and bag of money. He got dressed and climbed down the balcony that led to the pool area. He did not give a fuck about the bitches in his bed with whom he had good sex. Their good looks were not worth him going to jail.

The Feds were inside the hotel suite of the man whom they had just raided, and they were checking his information. He shared the same name as their suspect; however, they were of a different race and age.

"Sorry, Mr. Smith, for storming your room like this. We were given the wrong intel," the agent apologized as they exited the room and made their way to the real Ray Smith's room, which they had just received from the front desk.

With their levels of adrenaline already high, they moved in quickly and closed in on the room using another key card. They rushed inside the room with their guns out.

"FBI! Let me see your hands!" the agents yelled out as they closed in on the bedroom with the two sexy Latinas who were both naked.

The one closest to the Feds lay on her belly and exposed her perfect-looking ass and curves. The other lay on her side.

She showed how perky and picturesque her breasts were, just like the landing strip on her love spot.

"I guess he heard us down the hall, sir," the agent said, looking on at the naked Latinas and wishing he could be the guy in between them right then. However, he remained professional and asked, "You ladies have someone here with y'all last night?"

"*No habla Ingles, lo siento*," the Latina said with a smile.

The agent couldn't believe this shit.

"Get the Federales in here to translate," the agent yelled out.

Right then, the agent noticed in the girls' eyes that they knew exactly what he had just said.

"Oh, I get it, you no speaky the English. You speak Mexican prison for obstructing justice?" he said, which obviously got their attention.

"He no here anymore. Maybe he left when we sleeping," the female said.

The agents searched the room for clues that would give them a sense of the direction in which he headed, but nothing.

Ra Ra was running like a track star, trying to get as far away from the resort as fast as he could. Thoughts of going to jail added to the fuel that he needed to run harder. He was also wondering how the fuck they found him! Maybe someone at the resort recognized him? An employee? A tourist? Somebody recognized his face? It wasn't the women he was dealing with because he gave them fake names, except for one of them, Carmen, who had stood out to him. The same girl he was thinking about called as soon as he got far enough away to feel comfortable.

He ran a few more blocks before slowing down. He was breathing hard and sweating even harder. He walked over to a food truck.

"*Mira deme un* Coca-Cola, *por favor*?" Ra Ra said, taking out five American dollars and handing it to the Mexican man as he slid the Coke across the counter. "Keep the change."

"*Gracias, amigo*," the Mexican man said, appreciating the extra money.

"*De nada, viejo*," Ra Ra answered while drinking the soda and catching his breath before calling Carmen.

He made her aware that he was in need of a ride right away in order to get even further away from the resorts and tourist area. The Feds did not take too much time going deep into the ghettos of Mexico.

It was not too long before Carmen pulled up in her red Toyota Camry. Ra Ra got in, feeling good in the air conditioning and even better getting away from the area.

"*Papi, que pasol?* You okay?" she asked.

"I'm good now that you came to get me. Carmen, I need a place to lay low for a little. I'll pay you or whoever until I get my own place down here," he said.

"You can stay at my place. It's only me and my mother. Besides, we need the security and comfort of a man around the house."

Ra Ra smiled and looked on at his sexy Mexican mami. He very much appreciated her looking out for him.

Carmen stood five foot four and weighed a fit 125 pounds, with a body showing off her youthful tight stomach. Her curves flowed over her body in all the right places. Her sparkling gray eyes added to her allure with her beautiful smile of innocence, dimples, and long silky black hair. She was a natural beauty with an even more intriguing personality.

He pulled out $1,000 and handed it to her.

"This is for your troubles, and also to help you and your mother around the house."

"Gracias, papi, but this is a lot of money, you know?"

"I can't put a price on wanting to be in the good company of you and your mother."

She focused on the road while driving when his comment put a smile in her heart and on her face. She felt appreciated by someone as he was to her and her mother.

Ra Ra was an ATL balla, so he didn't mind giving her the money; besides, he wasted more than that in one night at the strip club. He viewed Carmen as a female he would love to keep around in his life and for some time. She was only twenty years old, and she knew what she wanted in life and where she wanted to be. He found out all of this during their first meeting when he picked her brain. It made him paranoid at first that she asked him so many questions, but she caught his attention, which is why she was the only female from whom he decided to get a phone number.

As they were driving to her mother's house, he took in all of the streets of Mexico and saw how they lived. Kids with guns were running wild and chasing people around. Bodies lay up against buildings; they were either too drunk to get up or dead from a cartel *sicario*'s bullet. He couldn't believe the worlds away the resorts were from here, especially with all of the cocaine coming from and through the country.

CHAPTER 8

AFTER A LONG day at the amusement park, Shari, Tommy, and the kids made it back to the hotel suite at 7:00 p.m.

"Tommy, you know my flight leaves at 9:00 p.m., right?"

"Then we should make good use of that time," he said with a smirk on his face.

"When will we see you again?"

"Soon! You know I'll send for you. It'll probably be another city, state, or country, but wherever I am, I'll reach out to you."

"You know I'll come to you wherever you are," she replied, giving him a kiss while caressing his neck with her manicured nails.

The kiss led to roaming hands over each other's bodies until their clothes came off, with love bites to his chest as her soft hands found him and stroked him to attention. They both enjoyed the moment of a quickie before showering so she could get ready to return home.

After they said their goodbyes, she made her way to the airport.

Tommy made his way back over to the projects to see his Miami rida, Kiss.

As he pulled into the projects where Kiss lived, he could hear bursts of gunfire going off as young niggas tried to take out Tre. He could see Tre spraying off a MAC-10 in different directions in between ducking behind cars and taking cover while trying to close in on some little niggas.

Tommy Guns dug Tre's swag, so he took out his Glock 40mm and squeezed off, taking out one of the young bucks and hitting him in the back and thrusting him forward. He then fired at another young buck who shifted his weapons toward him. The slugs fired and crashed violently into the young buck's face, tearing half of it off as the life instantly escaped him.

"I told y'all fools don't be coming around here! I run this hood!" Tre yelled out.

The crazy thing about the projects was that the cops did not come unless they were called or just so happened to be in the neighborhood. Even when no one was in harm's way, the constant gunfire made them come multiple times before—that and fireworks that kids would set off to see if the cops would come. But now they left it up to those who needed help to call.

Crazy, but it's as real as it gets!

Tre came up on one little nigga who was still breathing and pointed his gun at him just in case he tried some slick shit.

"You bitches, y'all think it's not real out here! I run this shit! You want to get down or what? If not, I don't want to see you in my hood ever again!" Tre shouted, taking the young nigga's gun.

He was hit in the shoulder and leg, so Tre let him go for now.

"Like I said, you want to get down, and I'll put you onto the game. But if you come back, I'm going to let my fiends put ya body in the dumpster!" Tre warned while watching the little nigga limp off. "Good looking, OG."

"Don't worry about it, my nigga. This is the life I live. Plus, I fucks with ya swag!" Tommy Guns said, looking around to see at least six crackheads carrying the dead niggas that he and Tre had just shot. They put them in the back of an old-ass Ford pickup truck.

"What the fuck them niggas doing?" he asked.

"I got the fiends on my payroll. I hit them with a quarter ounce and they share the shit, but they take the bodies to another project and dump them in the big green dumpsters. That's some real tiered shit, huh, OG?" Tre laughed.

"Yeah, it is! I ain't never seen no shit like this!"

"Back to business, I'm ready to get down with you. Let me run in the crib and get this paper," Tre said, ready to pick up so he could continue to secure his projects.

Tommy Guns made his way into the crib to secure the bricks for Tre. Kiss was upstairs being intimate with someone. He could hear her as he stood at the bottom of the steps. He laughed to himself knowing this was some funny shit, because she didn't even hear him come in. The crazy thing was that she knew Tommy had a key, so why take a chance? But that was Kiss. She was a ride-or-die type of chick.

"Ohhhhh, ohhhhh, ohhhhhh, right there! Give me that big dick! Mmmmmmmh, mmmmmh! Yes, yes, yes, give it to me! Mmmmmmmh!" she moaned and let out as some nigga was fucking her the long way.

Tommy didn't care as long as his money and product were cool. She could do her, just as he did him with his baby momma.

After Kiss and the mystery nigga were done doing them,

Tommy quietly sat on the couch and waited on her to come downstairs. He also had his trusted associate sitting in his lap—his fully loaded .44 Magnum that was all ready to go. He left his Glock in the car. He always felt that the Magnum up close and personal made a statement.

Kiss and her friend came down the steps and were both shocked to see him sitting there. Tommy Guns was pissed when he saw the nigga holding the same bags that Little D and Geez gave to him that contained the money and the ten bricks. He stood up from the couch and looked on at the nigga with murderous eyes.

"Yo, nigga, where the fuck do you think you're going with my shit?"

Before the lame-ass nigga could try to explain himself, Tommy squeezed the trigger and unleashed a thunderous round that roared through the air. The bullet slammed into the guy's chest and erupted his heart on impact while at the same time blowing a hole the size of a softball out his back. He was dead before his body even hit the ground. Being a ride-or-die chick, Kiss reacted just as fast when she saw the nigga she was just fucking fall back against the wall. She pulled out her nickel-plated .380 with the black grip and fired off rounds at Tommy. One of the reckless rounds went between his legs and grazed his inner right thigh.

She turned quickly and ran back up the steps as Tommy returned fire, sending slugs her way while trying to chase her down. He ran behind her and wanted to kill the bitch for her betrayal. As he turned up the steps, she stood at the top and fired rounds that slammed into his body and thrust him back down the steps. As he lay there still gripping the Magnum, he thought about how this bitch was really trying to take him out and under at the same time. If she killed him and took his money and product, America and the FBI would be thanking her for this shit.

Kiss disappeared out of sight, since she did not want to be hit from the slugs he was firing.

She came back into view firing off recklessly as another of her slugs hit him in the side. Tommy Guns now saw the end coming near, until his anger and rage pulled him through, when he fired off the last two slugs at the crazy bitch. The first of the slugs hit right above her nose, snapping her head back with brute force. It broke her neck while at the same time it breached her skull and ejected her brains out the other side. The other slug hit her in the breast, twisting her body and taking half of her breast off as the powerful slug tore through her body and assured her death even more. Her lifeless body fell down the steps onto him. He could not believe this was how their time ended. He slid from underneath her.

"Damn, Kiss, your sexy ass didn't have to go out like this while fucking with this lame-ass muthafucka here," he said, kicking the lifeless body of the nigga she was fucking.

He then grabbed both of the bags and made his way out of the crib. Tre was standing there ready to move out on anyone that came through the door if it wasn't him.

"OG, you good? Who did this shit?"

"That crazy bitch and her side nigga tried to take me for my money and work."

"I know you handled you shit killing fools."

"They dead as a muthafucka. Get ya fiends on that shit, little nigga," he ordered. He then added, "Have them set her spot on fire if you want. Here's five bricks for you. I'll be back in two weeks or sooner if you call my handle I gave you."

"I got cash for two of them right now, so take this bag. I

got you, OG. You already know I'ma hold you down to the fullest!" Tre said while watching Tommy Guns get into his whip wounded. "Stay focused, OG. That nigga and that bitch deserved what they got."

Tommy broke a smile through the pain that he was feeling from his wounds. He got it together enough to drive off and then call Tony the Ghost. Tony was at his multi-million-dollar estate on Star Island, which boasted over twenty thousand square feet of pure opulence.

"*Hermano, que pasol?*"

"I need your help, Tony!" Tommy began, with his voice sounding in pain as he was driving.

"What's the problem, hermano?"

"I got hit up twice. You know I can't just walk into a hospital being on the run. The Feds would be all over me."

"Say no more, amigo. Meet me at the club. I'll have my private doctor take a look at you."

"Good looking, Tony," Tommy said before hanging up the phone and driving over to Skyblue nightclub.

It wasn't open for business yet, being early in the day; however, he figured that a few staff members might be there getting things in order for the night. Tommy parked his car and waited for Tony to arrive. He thought about how Kiss really had tried to take him out of the game. If she was about him 100 percent, she would have made a great asset to the rising empire he was in the process of rebuilding.

It didn't take long for Tony and his men to get to the club to assist the person he viewed as a financial interest. Tommy stepped out of his stolen whip with the bag of money in one hand. His guys grabbed the bag while the doctor took a look at Tommy. He saw that he would need a better-prepared environment to continue aiding him.

"Tony, we can't do this out here," the doctor said.

"Take him inside then," he said. "The doctor knows best, hermano. He's going to fix you up real good. You'll be ready for war after he's done."

Tommy gave a brief smirk followed by a head nod after feeling the pain in his shoulder and side. But the graze to his inner thigh was a flesh wound that felt like a bad rug burn times ten.

"So tell me, amigo, who did this to you?"

"This bitch I was fucking with and her side nigga. They

tried taking my money and my work until he saw me. I killed both of them for this shit. That bitch shot me three times before I put her down," Tommy explained before bracing himself as the doctor worked his magic and pulled the bullets from his shoulder and leg. "I'm a survivor, Tony. I've been hit before. It only makes me stronger and driven to get this money out here."

"I like you, Tommy. I see potential in our business relationship. If you want to stay free out here, think about using one of my other doctors to change your look entirely, as well as your fingerprints. The fingerprints are the best. They'll never know who you are, even if they think they do," Tony said as he gave a light laugh at the thought.

"I didn't even know the fingerprint shit was a thing. I'm down for it if it can help keep our business relationship thriving without me having to look over my shoulder every day," Tommy said, knowing if he changed his face and fingerprints, it would be the greatest escape ever. "I need to secure a few things before we take care of the face and fingerprint thing. I want to make sure what we have going on stays on the right track. There is $300,000 in that bag right there. I owe you

$50,000 more. I'll have that in a day or less. I'll also take you up on the offer to leave the country when it's all said and done. Maybe if I lay low, I can pop up looking different."

Tommy was bracing for change, and becoming rich and powerful at the same time. He would now have to surround himself with people like Tony. As for his team, he fucked with his little niggas because they all were loyal to the end.

CHAPTER 9

THREE WEEKS LATER Tommy Guns found himself chilling at Tre's mom's crib. Tre figured he would look out for the OG since he blessed him with the product.

Tre's mom, Trina, thought Tommy was cute; plus she was feeling his gangsta swag backed by him being a boss. Trina stood five foot five and had brown skin. Her dark brown eyes added to her cat-like look and pretty smile backed by her white teeth. She weighed a thick 140 pounds, but her body still looked tight and good to Tommy.

Trina was in the kitchen working her magic and making soul food. She prepared fried whiting, baked macaroni with four cheeses, greens, cornbread, corn on the cob, and black-eyed peas. She handed Tommy and Tre a plate before turning to make her way back into the kitchen.

"Trina, where's the hot sauce at?" Tommy Guns asked.

"I'll bring it back out. Let me get y'all something to drink," she responded.

She came back in with drinks and looked really sexy to Tommy. She set down their drinks in front of them and turned to go get her plate.

"You keep walking like that all sexy and shit, and I'ma put this hot sauce all over you and eat you up with this cornbread," Tommy chuckled.

She laughed and then gave him a sensual look as she turned and headed back into the kitchen. The look also meant that he could look but not touch. It was also a promise they made to Tre so they would not mix business with pleasure. In the event Tre's business did not go right, it would make the personal thing even harder to deal with. Tommy was a man of his word, so he only kept it to flirting with her. She was fine with that. They all sat back and enjoyed the home-cooked meal full of flavor, love, and soul.

~ ~ ~

Back up in Atlanta, Geez and Little D were getting Tommy Guns's money together at the stash spot in the Thomasville projects. After they put the money into their book bags, they made their way outside to their Hayabusas with all their custom features and hidden compartments for their weapons, money, or whatever. On the chrome package, Geez even got the blue-and-red flames on the side. As they came out toward their bikes, Little D saw that his bike was knocked over on its side.

Immediately, he got pissed from feeling that he was disrespected.

"Which one of y'all bitch-ass niggas knocked my shit over?" Little D asked.

He looked around and searched the faces of the niggas standing around as well as the bitches, just in case there was a bitch he fucked or someone acting stupid out here.

A nigga unexpectedly popped up from behind a few cars down.

"It was me, nigga!"

"Yo, D, watch ya back! These niggas trying to hit us!" Geez yelled out while pulling out his gun.

Little D already had his gun in hand and started letting go, unleashing roaring rounds from the .45 Desert Eagle. Slugs slammed into the nigga's body so violently that it punched holes through him. At the same time, some of his insides from the force of the slug exited out the other end. He hit the ground seconds away from life as his heart and lungs were breached from the molten slugs that had hit him.

"That's for knocking my bike over, nigga!" Little D said before shifting his gun onto the nigga with whom Geez was shooting out.

He was trying to hide between the cars because Little D and Geez had him pinned down with the onslaught of slugs gunning for him.

Little D ran around the other side and ducked between cars while he snuck up on the nigga. He didn't even see Little D until it was too late.

"Look into the flash and smile, nigga! I gotcha!" Little D said as he came from behind the nigga.

He tried to turn fast and get a shot off, but Little D sent slugs into his body and face, dropping and killing him where he stood.

"You niggas should know better than to try to get at us out here! This is the life we live and die for!" Little D snapped while eyeing everyone who was still standing around.

"Them niggas don't look like they from around here, D."

"Yeah, I don't recognize them, and their family won't either!" Little D said after firing off another round into the already dead boy's face. "Yo, Geez, help me lift my bike back up," Little D requested.

"We going to have to get you something you can handle, my nigga," Geez said while helping him.

"Nah, nigga. They just got to stop hating on us out here,

that's all."

They hurried, revving up their bikes, and raced out of the projects. They knew the cops would be coming, and they didn't want to stick around for that. Besides, the hood wouldn't tell on them, because they, too, would be gone when the cops came. The niggas that got killed weren't even from the hood, so that was the end of their story and the hopes of having their murders solved.

Once Geez and Little D made it out of Georgia, they stopped to refuel and call Tommy Guns to let him know that they were on their way.

"What's good, little nigga?" Tommy asked after answering his phone.

"We on our way down to get at you since it's been awhile."

"I'm in the same area but down a few cribs. I'll give you the spot when ya get closer."

"Alright, my nigga. See you then," Geez said before hanging up the phone and getting back on the road.

They were focused on taking the game to another level with Tony, who was now looking out for Tommy Guns.

CHAPTER 10

DOWN IN MEXICO, Ra Ra was settling in with his new girlfriend, Carmen, and her mother, who welcomed him with open arms and love. They also catered to his every need, treating him like a young king. Ra Ra loved his newfound life and freedom out of the country. He did not miss the hood that made him, nor his old head, Tommy Guns, who blessed him and his team with the game.

Ra Ra, Carmen, and her mother were in the living room drinking cold Coronas and listening to music, until Carmen's uncle and associates arrived at the house. He immediately took notice of the American in his family's home. Carmen saw the look on her uncle's face, so she spoke up first.

"Uncle Hector, *ese es mi novio*, Ra Ra, *de America*."

Ra Ra stood up immediately after recognizing that her uncle and his presence displayed his power and position. He was definitely somebody, Ra Ra thought to himself. He quickly extended his hand out to shake her uncle's hand.

"Nice to meet you, Señor Hector."

Hector pulled Ra Ra close and spoke in a low tone that only

he could hear.

"Amigo, welcome to *mi familia*. If you hurt her, I will cut your heart out while it's still beating, just so you can feel the pain you caused her."

He patted Ra Ra on the shoulder and gave him a smile while looking him in his eyes. Normally Ra Ra would be offended, but this was a different time and place.

"She's in good hands; and as for her heart, that's in good hands, too," Ra Ra responded.

Hector shifted his attention to his niece and her mother.

"I dropped by to see how mi hermano's *esposa y hija* are doing. I see that you're in good company with this Americano. I want you to feel free to call me or stop by. You are welcome at my place, Rosita," Hector said while looking at Carmen's mom.

"You know being around you all and what it does to me and my memories of my husband. However, I'm okay with you stopping by as you do. If we need anything, we'll let you know," Rosita said, not wanting to go into details that would stir up old feelings.

"*No to lo video*, Carmen. If you need anything, *llamame*. I know your mom has her ways of doing things, but it's my job to make sure you and your mother are always taken care of," Hector said before kissing Rosita on the cheek and then Carmen before he and his men exited.

Ra Ra made his way over to the window and watched Hector and his men in a convoy of four black Range Rovers with tinted windows, which concealed the four men in each truck. They all boasted fully automatic weapons along with two 9mm handguns each. They were all ready to protect their boss.

"Really, your uncle is a boss in this country?" Ra Ra said after seeing the obvious.

"He's a very powerful man here in my country. He is respected by many and feared by even more. That's all I'll say for now."

She didn't need to say anything else. Ra Ra figured the rest out by himself.

Hector Guzman was Mexico's number one cartel boss, who took the position of El Chapo since a new power and face to fear was needed to keep the balance and distribution flowing into the US and around the world. Hector started off with his brother, until his brother got ambushed over a year ago and murdered by one of their rivals trying to gain position. Rosita never wanted to see the family or be part of that life anymore since it robbed her of the one love she ever had. Ramon Guzman was her high school sweetheart and the father of her only daughter, Carmen.

To avenge his brother, Hector captured those responsible and killed them in front of their entire families. He then killed each of their kids, and even their dog, before burning their bodies. They all drank tequila to celebrate as the bodies burned.

It was a day that shook the cartel world as those in Sinaloa, Juarez, and other areas were put on notice as to who was now in charge.

Hector stood five eleven and had thick eyebrows and a thick mustache on an otherwise clean-shaven face. His dark black eyes added to his murderous look. He did not take any shit from anyone. It was either his way or say goodbye to your life, because he was either taking it or would have his *sicarios* put a bullet in your head.

Ra Ra now thought about how he could connect the dots between her uncle back to the States, which would make his old head, Tommy Guns, proud of his networking skills. He just had to take it one step at a time. He did not want to approach Hector the wrong way or make him look past him dating his niece.

CHAPTER 11

BACK IN HARRISBURG, Federal agents were processing and transferring federal informant and witness, JD, to a safe house in Florida, far away from Pennsylvania.

Agent Johnson was also trying to track down all leads given to him in regard to Tommy Guns Anderson. But he was coming up short each time, which made him even more determined to catch the son of a bitch.

People in every hood across America all viewed Tommy Guns as a legend and one of their own, so those who did see him respected his gangster and would not report him. Others were starstruck by his presence. They knew that if they betrayed him, they would also end up dead. Agent Johnson also realized this with the length of time he had been on the run with the FBI and DEA using their resources to track him.

While Agent Johnson and his team focused on tracking down Tommy Guns, down in Florida, Little D and Geez pulled into the projects where Tommy Guns was with his young homie. Once they got off their bikes and walked up to him and Tre, Tommy introduced them to the boy.

"Little D and Geez, this is my young nigga Tre. He be putting in work out here and getting that money and laying anything down in his way to get a dollar. Ain't that right, little nigga?"

"You already know I'm about mine!" Tre responded before flipping up his shirt and displaying the 9mm automatic.

"What's good, Tre? I'm Geez, and this is Little D. So you getting this money with us, huh?"

"OG got at me after seeing that I get it done, so you know I'm about making that paper," Tre admitted.

In the middle of their conversation, a loud voice came through the air from a distance of roughly fifty or so yards. It immediately got all of their attention.

"Yo, Tre! You killed my baby brother, nigga! You gonna die fo' dat shit!"

The rapid back-to-back sound of a 9mm Uzi on a three-burst switch sounded off loud as bullets crashed into the cars and projects around them as the shooter started to move in on them. At the same time, the shooter tried to evade the slugs that were being fired back at him from Tommy and his gang.

When the cat saw that he had four guns aimed and shooting

at him, he decided to bounce and try the shit another time when Tre did not have a team with him. He took off running toward the car he had parked a few blocks away.

"That nigga's mine next time he comes through here acting like he about that life," Tre said with a pissed-off attitude. "He can join his brother in the muthafucking ground."

"Calm down, my nigga. He ain't coming back here seeing how we deep. Let's go in the crib to take care of business," Tommy suggested.

Once in the crib, they continued talking about what had happened and what led to Tre killing the dude's brother. Then the conversation shifted to more serious business at hand. Tommy was giving the little niggas game on how he wanted to expand.

"Tre, Geez, Little D. We about to make a power move with this nigga Tony. He's connected on another level which makes us connected to him. Now, Tre, I want you to see what you can do in the city outside your projects. Spread out in other projects to distribute more work. Geez and Little D, y'all niggas expand in Georgia and the Carolinas to see what y'all can do there. When this shit comes through, we going to have to move it, because this nigga Tony is the real deal, feel me?"

"We got you, OG," Tre said, all ready to get to a dollar.

"We can even expand to ya city. See what that money and them shawties like up there," Geez said.

"There's some real special dime pieces that will have your mind fucked up, my niggas," Tommy said. "But on some real shit, if y'all niggas stick with me and stay loyal 'til the end, the sky is the limit. Because this nigga Tony, from what it looks like, is going to take us there."

Tommy stopped speaking when his cell phone sounded off. He didn't recognize the number and normally would not answer, but he did after seeing that it was an out-of-town number.

"Yo, what's good?"

"*Que pasa*, homes?"

"Who the fuck is this?"

"It's me, my nigga!" Ra Ra said while laughing and fucking with Tommy.

"Oh shit, it's the homie Ra Ra!" Tommy said, tapping the phone and placing it on speaker so the crew could hear the call. "Yo, Ra Ra! I got Little D and Geez here plus my new little nigga, Tre, from Miami."

"What it do, folk? How y'all niggas doing up there?" Ra Ra asked.

"We chasing that money down," Little D said.

"I miss y'all niggas, man. I wish I could be there. Y'all should come down and see this country how I'm seeing it," he said, meaning the cartels and other shit behind the tourist scene.

"Don't worry, my nigga. I'm working on something major that could get you back here safe," Tommy Guns said.

"I ain't gonna say much over this line, but I'm in traffic myself. You would be proud of this move, my nigga."

"Yo, Ra Ra! I know you getting them sexy-ass Spanish mamis down there!" Little D said, all hyped up and wishing he was there.

"Yeah, I met a few, but there was one that slowed me down," Ra Ra said while Carmen spoke up in the background.

"*Esta ahora*, papi!" she said, all ready to go.

Little D, Geez, Tommy Guns, and Tre all heard her, and they laughed at the homie.

"Whoa! Whoa! What's going on down there, Ra Ra?" Geez asked.

"I told y'all niggas I found the right one. Trust me on this. I'm about to go out with my lady and her folks. I'm a get at y'all later, alright?"

"Be safe, my nigga, and do you with one or all of the women," Geez said.

After the call ended, Tommy decided to take his men to get something to eat at the Chinese spot across town to show his appreciation as well as to continue grooming his team.

CHAPTER 12

TWO HOURS AFTER cramming their faces with shrimp-and-pork egg rolls, pork-and-shrimp fried rice, crab legs, and other fresh Chinese food, they all made their way out of the buffet. Little D spotted something that stood out to him.

"OG Tommy, that looks like them alphabet boys in that Crown Vic over there!" Little D called out.

Tommy's attention went straight toward the car at which his little nigga was pointing. His heart and mind picked up its pace. He thought that they were about to close in on him, so he started looking around to see if he noticed anyone else in an unmarked car. Nothing. What the fuck is going on here? Tommy thought as he jumped into the car. Little D and Geez got on their bikes and waited to see what their old head was about to do. Tre was in the whip with Tommy.

Two Federal agents exited the vehicle followed by a third person who slid out of the back seat of the Crown Vic. Tommy and Tre were lying low behind the dark-tinted windows of the 760Li BMW as they watched the agents approach the entrance of the buffet.

"You got to be kidding me!" Tommy Guns said after seeing who the third person was who exited the Fed's car. That rat muthafucka JD! he thought. "This nigga is a rat with nine muthafucking lives."

"Who the fuck is that nigga, OG?" Tre asked.

"That bitch-ass muthafucka is the reason I'm on the run. He set me up with the Feds to cop some bricks, and that nigga turned out to be a Federal agent. I killed that Fed nigga, just like I'ma kill this piece of shit."

The Feds flew in JD to relocate him; however, unbeknownst to any of them, this was the city where their number-one fugitive had chosen to run.

Tommy wanted to jump out of the car right then, but he had a better idea of how he was going to get that muthafucka for his betrayal. Tommy now flashed back to when he shot up JD in Harrisburg and how he survived to tell the Feds about the Range Rover he had in Candy's name. The thoughts of that alone pissed him off, because his nigga Fat Money lost his life that day.

He sat back and planned his next move while the rat-ass nigga was inside feeding his face, unaware that he was enjoying his last meal.

A little over an hour had passed by and the Feds, along with their CI, left the Chinese buffet with full bellies ready to hit the road to get to the safe house. They got into their car and filled out their travel log before pulling off and leaving the parking lot, not knowing that they were being followed. They drove over four blocks and came to a red light while making small talk about the food they had just eaten. They never saw the two motorcycles pull up on the driver and passenger sides, until both bikes stopped. Each agent looked at the rider on their side of the car, only to be greeted with a barrage of bullets that slammed into their faces and instantly sucked the life from them.

"Oh, my fucking God! He's here! It's the fucking devil himself!" JD yelled out after seeing the agents killed in true gang-land style.

Fear swept over him when he saw the motorcycles take off and leave him there alone—or so he thought.

Tommy Guns quickly pulled up in his BMW and rolled down the dark-tinted windows as he closed in on the back passenger side of the Crown Vic. JD instantly saw the darkness in Tommy Guns's eyes right before the flash of fire from him squeezing the trigger on his .44 Magnum. Two slugs raced out of the gun and slammed into his skull, ejecting his brains throughout the interior of the car and leaving him dead and unable to betray or infiltrate anyone else's organization or empire. Tommy pulled off after mashing the gas and forcing the V12 engine to thrust power into the car, which allowed him to escape from the sirens he could hear approaching.

CHAPTER 13

THE NEXT MORNING, Federal agents were flaming while thinking that there was a mole in their agency that leaked the location of their confidential informant (CI) that led to their agents and the CI being murdered gang-land style.

The Harrisburg FBI office was now under scrutiny from Jack Ross for this slap in their face. Agent Johnson was the first to speak in defense of his office.

"Sir, we've been tracking Mr. Anderson for so long that we may have forced him right where our CI was to be located. Maybe it was pure coincidence that they crossed paths, if that's the case."

"Are you kidding me, Johnson? This is one hell of a coincidence! Maybe I'll try my luck at the lottery since luck is in the air!" Ross said sarcastically and pissed off at the same time. "Now all of this has to be explained to the press, who are all over this incident with the dead agents. We need to run Tom Anderson's picture again and what he could look like now. We need to take this son of a bitch down!" Jack said before he paused and looked around the office to see if there was a mole assisting Tommy Guns with information that led to killing the one person who originally helped bring him down. If there was a mole, this could explain how he'd been on the run so long. Someone could be allowing him to know the Feds' every move?

Jack's thinking was starting to become paranoid.

"I guess nothing can get done around here unless I do it myself," he said sarcastically.

Agent Johnson looked on at his boss. He did not want to say anything because it would only add fuel to the fire.

Meanwhile back in Florida, the images of the two dead agents and CI were all over the news as well as in the newspapers.

Tommy was at Tre's crib watching the news while Geez, Little D, and Tre were messing with the motorcycles. Tre was also outside hustling in between checking out the bikes.

Tommy made a call to Tony the Ghost so they could arrange a face-to-face conversation about business, so the call was brief and to the point. Tommy made it outside and got his squad together to head to Miami's seaports where over a million tons of cargo came through each year, including the finest cocaine from Colombia.

"Yo, little niggas! Get y'all shit together so we can get ready to go holla at the connect," Tommy said, trying to get the crew in order.

Geez and Little D jumped on their bikes and followed behind Tommy and Tre in the car.

Once they arrived at the ports, Tommy pulled up to where Tony was still keeping his brother's legacy alive with the color scheme of sky blue. The custom sky-blue Rolls Royce Phantom's plush white leather was just as clean as Tony as he stepped out of the car with his goons exiting the trucks. He also had another sexy-ass Latina on his side, who was boasting a chrome 9mm with a silencer and white pearl handle.

Tommy Guns came up with his team and approached Tony. He was ready to take care of business. He extended the bag of money containing $300,000 in it.

"This is what I have toward our new business deal and relationship," Tommy explained.

"I like you, Tommy. You have done something that most men wouldn't have done being on the run from the law. You didn't make any excuses as to why you couldn't pay. You just paid, and now you're ready to continue doing business, which is a good sign of how your future will turn out. I like your drive, hermano. You have the hunger in you," Tony said before he paused to allow Tommy to take it all in. "Now we can start building this empire you spoke of."

"Since I'm dealing directly with you, Tony, the price should be lower than thirteen a key."

Tony began laughing at Tommy's angle to negotiate the price that his brother had given to him. He looked over at his goons and then back to Tommy.

"Okay, eleven and a half is my set price for you with the quantity. It won't change unless I lose a shipment or something goes wrong with business."

"I think that's a good price point. Now let's talk quantity."

"Your number is fifty, hermano, until you can show me you can get rid of more."

"Now that we have the business side of things secured, I want to take you up on your offer to change my look with your surgeons—the fingers and all. This new look and identity will allow me to grow in this business without looking over my shoulders for the Feds."

"*Llamame mañana, hermano.* We'll go over business and your new look then."

"Tony, I really appreciate you seeing my hunger and drive."

"I have an eye for shit like this, and you deserve this chance and a new look," Tony said after getting back into his car and allowing the convoy to take off to its next business deal.

CHAPTER 14

TWO MONTHS LATER Rakman Hussein was preparing to go to court to be tried for multiple murders and acts of terror against the country. He was in the reception shakedown area of the prison putting on his court clothes, a bullet-proof vest, and handcuffs provided by FBI agents who were escorting him to the downtown Federal courthouse. Once the agents secured him, they exited the prison, which was on high alert since the incident with Tommy Guns in York, Pennsylvania. They also had to maintain a high alert since a man of his stature may have Muslim followers who would attempt to get him out.

Four all-black Yukon Denalis awaited in the sally port, with each one boasting four agents inside armed and ready to secure the package to get him to the courthouse safe and sound. They also had the FBI's chopper in the sky watching over them just in case shit went wrong.

The convoy of trucks exited the prison as radio chatter among the agents continued, with all eyes on the package in tow. They came upon a red light while driving on Paxton Street, so all the vehicles halted yet remained on full alert. Then it happened. All of their radio communications want silent, and all electronics in the trucks also shut down. At the same time, the helicopter's electrical power went down, which forced an abrupt landing in the Harrisburg East Mall parking lot. No cars or buildings using electricity within one hundred yards could use it at that very moment.

A silent sonic boom suddenly hit with a wave of powerful air that shattered all of the windows on the four Yukon Denalis, exposing Rakman Hussein and all four agents. Immediately following the abrupt blast, covert-like operatives came from every angle. Silenced tranquilizer darts hit their targets with trained precision, taking down each Federal agent and knocking them unconscious within seconds of being hit.

At the same time and speed, they rushed in on the truck with Rakman and removed him to an awaiting vehicle that was not affected by the electronic shutdown. They made their getaway as if they were not even there. The Federal agents never saw this coming; and even though they saw operatives coming, they had no chance to think or react that fast.

Thanks to his powerful and connected associates, Rakman was now a free man.

Meanwhile, there was a $2 million reward out for Tommy Guns Anderson. The FBI announced a GoFundMe account they put together for all of the victims in the wake of the murderer's path. They figured this would bring him in a lot faster than chasing behind him. At the end of the day, people were more loyal to money than anything else, and the FBI figured that those in the streets and hoods of America would eventually turn on him.

Jack Ross stood in front of a slew of cameras preparing to address the nation on this matter. He wanted to give people the incentive to come forward with Tommy Guns's location.

"To all of you out there who helped raise this money, trust that this reward is going to good use. Whoever can bring in this man, by giving us any information that leads to his arrest and conviction, will be rewarded with $2 million. If you have any information, don't be afraid to call the 1-800 number on the bottom of your screen," Jack announced before turning around and pointing at the wives and children of the murdered agents. "These people here, America, are counting on you to bring the monster in who took their loved ones."

~ ~ ~

Tommy Guns was in New York City at the Roosevelt Hotel in Manhattan in his suite watching the crazy shit on the news and laughing at Jack Ross's speech. He got up from the chair and walked over to the mirror. He looked in it at his new face thanks to Tony's doctor.

"They'll never find you, my nigga," he said as he looked on with a smile.

Tommy laughed until his cell phone sounded off. He saw that it was his young nigga Little D.

"What's good, my nigga?" Little D said.

"Ain't shit! I'm sitting here trippin' off of the news with this Fed nigga talking about me."

"Yo, OG, I just got off of the phone with Geez. He said something about your little man getting hit by a car or something," Little D said.

Geez was in Harrisburg holding it down while getting money and fucking chicks out there. He loved the way they did their thing, with no strings attached.

"What? Who hit my son? Which son is it?"

"I think he said little Tommy. Call your folks to confirm this shit."

"Say no more. I'm on it. I'll get back to you when I take care of this shit," he said before hanging up the phone and looking in the mirror full of anger.

Tommy Guns also changed his name to Charles Warren, and he had the credentials and fingerprints to back him all the way. The only people who were aware of his facial and ID transition were those in his circle and Tony's people, none of whom would say a word. They knew that their lives would be at stake from Tony or Tommy Guns.

Tommy left the hotel suite and headed downstairs to leave. The valet arrived with his new sky-blue CL65 AMG Mercedes Benz coupe with the V12 engine, the same as Turnpike Tito's, his old business associate. He, too, was keeping his legacy alive and well, because the sky was truly the limit when you're in the game this far and money is flowing in by the boxes.

"Here's your car, Mr. Warren. Have a nice day, sir," the valet said, obviously working for his tip.

Tommy Guns gave him a $50 bill since he wasn't at the hotel but for two days on business.

Once he was in the car, he made his way through the Lincoln Tunnel and headed back to Pennsylvania to a city he had not been to in a while. At the same time, he thought about who had hit his kid and how bad he was injured. A part of him was now feeling like John Gotti when his boy got hit. He, too, wanted to kill the muthafucka who ran over his son.

CHAPTER 15

CLOSE TO THREE hours had passed before Tommy made his way into Harrisburg, after merging onto I-83 and getting off at the 17th Street exit on the Hillside side of the city. He immediately focused on driving to Shari's crib to get to his son, since she did not answer her phone when he called multiple times on his drive down to the city, which pissed him off even more. He did not know if she was at the house or the hospital, which made him even more anxious to get to the city and to her house.

"I miss this fucking city!" he said while looking around while driving through the city on his way to Shari's crib.

Tommy called up Geez to see where he was so he could meet him over by Shari's spot.

"G's up!" Geez said while answering the phone.

"G's up, what's good, little nigga. I'm here in the city on my way over to my BM's crib. Meet me over that way, alright?"

"I got you. I'm up in ya old hood right now getting to it, but I'm on my way in your direction," Geez said. He hung up and took care of BI, knowing he had to make sure all was good with his OG and his son.

As the call ended, Tommy pulled up to Shari's crib and looked around as always to make sure that no Fed boys were in sight. Nothing. He parked, turned off the car, and then sat briefly for a few seconds to see if anything would come of his presence. Nah, if the Feds were there, they would be closing in by now, he thought.

He exited the vehicle and walked up to the door while still looking around to make sure there were no stick-up niggas trying to get the drop on him either. He knocked across the door a few times and then tried the doorbell. Shari came to the door with a concerned look on her face, which in his eyes meant something really bad was wrong with his son.

"Can I help you with something?" she asked, not recognizing him or his new face.

Hearing her ask this also threw him off a little because he forgot in the moment, thinking about his son, that he had a new look of which she was not aware.

"Shari, stop playing with me! It's Tommy," he whispered to her.

"Huh? If you're really him, tell me—!"

"Miami Hilton," he responded, knowing she would not be able to forget the freaky sex they had during the time they spent together as a family.

She let him ramble on about his new look, but his attention shifted to her mother in the kitchen, who looked back at him as if he was the devil himself. Her mother never liked him one bit, which also put a strain on their relationship when they were together.

Shari came up and hugged him, but it was different. She was acting strange, Tommy thought. Her words did not match her actions.

"You know I'll always love you no matter what. We have our babies to love and bond with," Shari said, now placing fear that something really wrong was going on or had gone on.

"What's going on, Shari? Where's my son at?" he asked, thinking that something bad had happened to him.

She immediately began to cry and apologize.

"Sorry, it's not my fault, Tommy," she said while pulling away from his hug and then looking into his eyes.

In that very moment, he thought that his son was dead, so a wave of anger came across him. He wanted to make someone pay for this. Then it happened. Almost forty agents stormed into the house from the back entrance, the front entrance, and upstairs. They all closed in on Tommy Guns Anderson, making sure he did not have a chance to pull out his gun or even slip through their grasp anymore.

"Mr. Anderson, you're under arrest, thanks to your girl here. You're not going to get away this time. I do like the new face, but it won't do you any good behind bars. But you'll have a mirror to look in and realize how much you fucked up in this free world!" the agent said as he aggressively placed the cuffs on him.

"You fucked up a good thing, Shari! You don't even know what the fuck you just did!" Tommy snapped.

"I'm sorry! I'm sorry, Tommy."

"You dumb bitch!" he yelled while looking into her eyes.

Right in that very moment, she could see the killer in him that everyone else had seen before they met their demise.

Shari's mom came out from the kitchen with a knife in her hand.

"You don't be cussing at my daughter like you done lost your damn mind!"

"Ma'am, you can't be doing this. We have everything under control here," the agents said before closing in and disarming the knife.

They then took hold of her and allowed her to come to her senses before they would have to take her to jail, too.

Shari's mom did not know about the stash that Tommy had in the house, or she would have convinced her daughter to take it.

"I never liked your black ass for my daughter anyway!" Shari's mom expressed.

"Shari, you and your mom are now dead to me! No love!"

The agents escorted Tommy outside to the car and took him to jail where he would face the federal death penalty for the murder of Agent Cornick and the others, if they could prove it.

As he was being put into the back seat of the car, Geez arrived in his Porsche Cayenne truck just in time to see that his old head was being taken in by a slew of Feds around him. Not good. At that moment, Geez knew that Tony was going to want his money no matter what took place. He might even send a hit out on the arresting agents just to get his point across. As soon as Geez passed by the car with Tommy in the back seat, he could see him looking back at him. Geez was ready to move out for his old head no matter what. The MAC-11 was already fully loaded. He knew he could catch them off guard and take out as many as he could to give his old head a chance to get out of the Feds' car. Instead, Tommy shook his head no. He knew he was clearly outnumbered. Besides, the Feds came prepared for war this time, with agents standing around with their guns out and their MP5s ready to go.

Geez did not want to leave his old head behind. When he came to his senses, he immediately called up Little D.

"Geez, what's up, folk?" Little D answered on the second ring.

"They got Tommy Guns!" Geez said.

He was hurt and pissed at the same time, because he felt helpless and unable to do anything about it as he passed by.

"Get the fuck outta here! How the fuck did that happen?"

"I think this bitch he got used his son to set him up. How else would the Feds know where he was or when he was coming? That bitch must have lied about their son!" Geez said, thinking about putting a bullet in Tommy's baby mom's head for this shit.

But first he would have to confirm this with Tommy Guns to make sure that was exactly what had taken place.

"Yo, I'ma hit up Tre to put him onto this shit."

"Be easy and stay up, Geez."

"You already know, my nigga," he said, before hanging up and making the next call to Tre.

They all knew what needed to be done in case this type of shit took place. Tommy made them aware of this just in case a day came and he was not around. He just did not think that day would be today.

CHAPTER 16

JACK ROSS HAD just been made aware of the arrest of Tommy Anderson. It made him feel good to have this monster taken down on his watch; and at the same time, it gave some closure to the families he had affected.

Now with Tommy Guns behind bars, he had to focus on Rakman Hussein and the elaborate jailbreak that was not of the norm. This was well planned and carried out by trained elites to have taken out sixteen agents yet sparing each of their lives.

When the slew of police officers, state troopers, and Federal agents arrived on the scene where the sixteen agents were taken down, they were briefed on what they could recount until they went unconscious from the tranquilizer darts.

"The device used to take out our communications was not something you'd find at RadioShack. This shit was high tech and used by our government for many reasons, not to compromise our federal agency with this jailbreak."

Joe Davis, the assistant director of the Harrisburg office, was concerned about his men, so he responded to the chopper pilot's statement.

"This is an act of terror against our agency. The men that did this are well trained and covert. All the technology used here was backed by skill and precision. They didn't want you guys dead; they only wanted Rakman Hussein, and they got him with ease."

After Joe gave his views on what took place, he started walking around the scene looking for something that would show who these trained men were, but he found nothing. He needed something to report back to Jack Ross.

~ ~ ~

At 6:01 p.m. all the major news outlets and social media sites were plastering information about Tommy Guns's arrest. Jack Ross was now in Harrisburg dealing with Rakman's escape. Agent Johnson was also with him at his side as he spoke to the press.

"Yes, we have finally captured the man who has brought fear into this country and grief into the homes of the agents we've lost. Thanks to Agent Johnson and his men, along with the tips we've received, we were able to bring down this monster. I know you guys have a ton of questions, so I'll take a few."

The questions flew rapidly until he focused in on one reporter at a time, giving each one their fair shot to ask a question.

"This question is for you, Mr. Ross. You've captured Mr. Anderson, but Rakman Hussein managed to escape from the custody of sixteen armed and trained federal agents who were taken out by tranquilizer darts. Who could possibly have this power to take out all of those agents as well as to down the helicopter following them?"

This was the first time Mr. Ross was made aware of the details of Rakman's escape.

"No comment until I gather more info on this situation," Jack responded before turning to Agent Johnson and stepping away from the microphones. He then leaned into Johnson and said, "I need you to get behind this. Find out more information. The press shouldn't know more than I do. It's insane."

Jack Ross continued on with his press conference and provided answers to a few of their questions.

Meanwhile down in Florida, Tony the Ghost was watching the news and saw what the rest of America was seeing with the press conference announcing the capture of Tommy Guns. This alone made him upset because he just had given Tommy a large shipment. Tony figured that someone must have set him up for the $2 million reward. He wanted to find out exactly who was responsible for this, and he wanted to reach out to one of his associates that would get him that information.

"*Oye, yo necessito telefono,*" Tony called out.

A member of his staff immediately came over and handed him the cordless phone.

"Anything else, señor?"

"Bring me a double shot of peach Cîroc."

"Right away, señor."

Tony made the call to his associate who would have the answers that Tony needed; and if not, he would get them.

The phone picked up on the third ring.

"*Hola, que tal?*"

"*Viejo*, we have a problem that needs to be fixed," Tony said before going into full detail on what was going on.

His associate assured him that it would be taken care of.

"I'll have my people look into this. I hope it doesn't offset anything we have in progress," the man over the phone said.

"No, no! Everything is just fine," Tony replied, assuring his powerful friend that he had everything under control.

"No more calls like this. It's not good for business, and it's not a good look for you running the business," the bossy voice said over the phone before hanging up, not even giving Tony a chance to respond.

Once the call ended, the bossy voice over the phone turned to his sicarios in his presence.

"*Mira yo tengo trabajo para ti.*"

Meanwhile, back at his mansion, Tony was drinking the double shot of peach Cîroc his staff had brought to him. All he could do was think about the call he just had with his powerful associate. Tony also wanted resolve.

"Oye, I want you to go over to the projects and bring me back Tommy Guns's crew. I need to speak with them *ahora!*" Tony said to his security.

His men did just as he requested. He knew business still had to be conducted even with Tommy being in jail. Tony wanted his money or his product.

~ ~ ~

Jack Ross was being briefed on the Rakman escape at 8:04 p.m. He was taken aback by what he had heard thus far, because this was not done by regular men trying to break someone out. This was a covert extraction carried out with precision.

"Okay, men, keep a tight seal on this thing until I reach out to my superiors," Jack Ross said as he began to make the necessary calls around the nation to see who was responsible for this.

The first call he made was to the National Security Association (NSA). They neither knew anything nor admitted to anything. Regardless, nothing came from that call. He then called the Counter Terrorist Division (CTD), and they, too, had nothing to say about the incident. Jack was now getting frustrated because he figured he would have at least gotten somewhere by reaching out to these elite agencies, but nothing so far. He called up the CIA, and that led to another dead end and cold shoulder. Every agency seemed to turn its back on him and what had taken place, especially at the mention of Rakman Hussein's name.

About fifteen minutes after he had made his last call, Jack's phone began to ring. An anonymous number displayed on the screen. But when he answered the call, he realized it was someone from one of the agencies he had just called.

"Mr. Ross, if you want to know what I know, meet me on the I-83 bridge, and come alone. I'll be there in exactly thirty minutes. If you miss it or I sense that something is wrong, I'm gone and you will never have the information that you're in search of."

Click. The phone hung up leaving Jack Ross on high alert as his mind raced while trying to figure out what was happening and why the secrecy when speaking about Rakman Hussein and the escape. He wanted answers, so he needed to get there on time and alone. Jack Ross looked at his watch and saw he had twenty-nine minutes to get to his destination or he was going to miss out on something that could crack the case wide open and lead to Rakman Hussein and the men who assisted in getting him out.

About twenty-eight minutes later, Jack pulled onto the bridge behind a car on the right side that he saw with its hazard lights on. A lone man got out of the vehicle and walked around to the other side, away from the oncoming traffic. He looked over the Susquehanna River and thought about what he was going to tell Jack Ross.

Jack exited his car and then made his way over to the intriguing, well-dressed man.

"Jack, my name is Richard O'Neil from the CTD. I used to be the director of operations for the CIA as well. I was responsible for dictating where foreign operatives went to retrieve intel from other countries—spies to be exact."

"Agent O'Neil, tell me what the hell we are doing right here!"

"Rakman Hussein knows people who are connected to those in powerful places. I'm talking about governors, senators, and presidents, and not just in this country, but those around the world."

"So you're telling me the people that got him out of jail are on our side?" Jack questioned in disbelief.

"It's exactly what I'm saying."

"I need names. Be more specific so I can help put a face to this thing to expose them for the traitors they are!" Jack said with anger.

Agent O'Neil looked out at the river and heard the clashing of the water beneath the bridge running over the little dam below. At the same time, he heard the fast cars drive by behind him. As he was processing his thoughts and the names of those he was about to tell Jack Ross, he halted in mid-thought. Jack Ross immediately could see the pink mist spraying from the side of Agent O'Neil's head followed by the crack and boom of the sniper rifle that had fired the gun. His brains immediately ejected out the side of his head onto his car, snapping his neck from the brute force of the gun as his body fell to the ground.

The shot was fired from a distance, yet Jack figured with the time it took to hear the crack of the gun to when O'Neil was hit, it was an incredibly accurate shot. Jack was on the ground fast, since he did not want to be next. His heart was beating just as fast as his mind was racing. He tried to figure out what the hell he had gotten himself into. He got it together and quickly crawled to the other side of the car, where he opened his door and got inside. He remained low, knowing a sniper could easily take him out. He quickly drove off and realized that the situation was far more serious than he had expected. Who could he trust if anyone with what little information he had learned from Agent O'Neil? Jack was also aware that elite agencies could track his whereabouts, so he grabbed his cell phone and prepared to toss it out of the window when it started to ring. He answered nervously.

"Hello! Jack Ross here."

"Mr. Ross, be careful of the questions you ask or the people you associate yourself with. If you think you know something or have information, rid yourself of those thoughts before a sniper bullet clears your mind without you seeing it coming," the voice on the other end of the phone said before hanging up.

In fear, Jack tossed the phone out onto the highway and allowed the cars behind him to run it over multiple times. He made his way back home to Maryland. He was full of emotions and confusion as he tried mentally to embrace that Agent O'Neil had been murdered in front of him by a sniper's bullet.

How did they know he was going to be there in that exact location? Could they have been listening in on his calls the whole time, just waiting to see who he was going to meet? Jack had so many questions and thoughts tormenting his mind. He looked around as he drove fast down the highway, and he feared any car that matched his speed while pulling up alongside him. He just wanted to get home and see his family. He'd had enough of this shit for one night.

CHAPTER 17

MEANWHILE BACK IN Miami, Geez and Little D were on their way to Tre's crib to take care of business. As they approached the crib, they noticed four H2 Hummers parked out front side by side.

"Yo, D, ain't that Tony's people in them trucks?" Geez asked while eyeing the trucks to see if anyone was inside of them. Nothing.

"Yo, nobody is in there," Little D said. "They in Tre's crib. Where else could they be?" he said while knocking on the door.

Trina came to the door with a look that meant something was wrong; but before they could react, Tony's goons came into view. Little D and Geez already had their guns aimed at the niggas thinking that something was wrong with Tre since they did not see him.

"What the fuck is going on, fool?" Little D blurted out while gripping his Glock 40mm.

"Yo, Tre, you up in there?" Geez asked, trying to look past the big Latino.

"*Tranquillo*, amigos. Jefe wants to talk to you guys about

Tommy. This isn't about gunplay. If it was, you would already have been dealt with."

They didn't trust the Spanish niggas, plus they still didn't see Tre.

"If everything is good, where's my nigga Tre at?"

"He's right here, mi amigo," the goon said, stepping aside and allowing Tre to exit the crib, all ready to meet Tony.

"I'm good, y'all. Plus, if there was beef, you know my hood ain't gonna let these niggas roll up in here like that."

The goons looked on at Tre, not liking what he said. But they did see many young thugs in the hood standing by strapped and ready to protect all the movement of drugs and money being made.

They all got into the Hummers ready to meet the boss. Tony awaited their arrival on the other side of the city at one of his many warehouses used for his import and export business.

When they finally arrived at the warehouse, they entered with Tony's goons right behind them. They saw Tony sitting at a table in the middle of the warehouse with two twin-looking Latinas, both of whom had bleached-blonde hair, baby-blue eyes, light skin, and perky breasts and were wearing sky-blue, tight dresses by DKNY that hugged every curve. Just like everyone else, the ladies were strapped with twin .380s and ready to roll. Tony remained calm with all of his power and protection as the young, street, thugged-out drug dealers approached him. He got straight to the point as each of them stood in front of the table.

"How did my friend Tommy get made?"

"I think it's that bitch he got the kids with. She called me saying that her son got hit by a car. I called Tommy and told him. He was in New York. He came down to be greeted with that shit. I wanted to help him, but there was too many of them Fed boys," Geez explained.

"What's her name?" Tony calmly asked while fondling his Cuban cigar between his fingers.

"Shari is her first name. I don't know her last name," Geez responded. "She lives on North Street. I don't know the exact address."

"It's obvious the kids don't mean anything to her, just as they don't mean anything to me since she has fucked with my money."

The crew became silent as they looked on at Tony puffing

on his cigar in thought.

"So, which one of you has my $1.5 million from the shipment I gave him? You are all on his team, so you are all responsible for my money," Tony said.

Tony gave Tommy three hundred kilos at 11.5 each. It came out to $1,450,000. Tony just rounded it off to the nearest number for the inconvenience. The money they had was Tony's because Tommy didn't even touch the three hundred kilos because he still had product left over from the last go-round.

"I have $150,000 for you," Geez said.

"I got $120,000, too," Little D said.

"I can get you fifty stacks right now," Tre lied, because he didn't want to give up Tommy's money so freely.

He would rather wait to see if Tommy sent them a message to get the shit from the stash house. They could then give it all back to Tony, not that he would take it back since he was all about money and no excuses.

"Get what you can and bring it back to me here. Don't make me wait too long for my money. It won't be good for you," Tony threatened while puffing his cigar and blowing the smoke out in a thick cloud.

"Tre, Geez, and I have to shoot back up to Atlanta where we keep everything, but on the motorcycles it shouldn't take long getting back here," Little D said.

"I take it I'll have to trust you two as I have done Tommy. Don't fuck this up! Time is money, so be here at 9:00 in the morning."

"We'll be here with the money in hand," Geez said.

"You all can leave me now," Tony said as he stood up from his chair.

The two women closed in on him and caressed his arms, affectionately catering to the boss.

Geez, Tre, and Little D were not feeling what had just taken place as they made it back to the Hummers that took them back to the projects. They had to come up with more than what they all had together. They knew this nigga wouldn't settle for less.

CHAPTER 18

AT 9:02 THE next morning, Geez, Little D, and Tony's men arrived back at the warehouse, minus Tre. Tony took notice of his absence while at the same time feeling disrespected by the young thug.

"*Hermanos, donde tu amigo?*"

"I don't know. He didn't answer his phone either. He's probably still asleep from staying up all night trying to get your money together," Geez said, not wanting to shit on the homie but giving him the benefit of the doubt.

Little D took his bag of money and walked it over to Tony before taking his place beside Geez, who also gave up a bag of money. Tony briefly looked into the bags and eyed the amount.

"Nice doing business with you, gentlemen," he said as he stood up from his chair while escorted by the two killa Latinas strapped with their twin .380s ready to rock out if need be.

Geez and Little D looked on as the nigga tried to figure out why he got up on that note. Tony looked over his shoulder back at his men.

"*Mata lo!*" he said, giving the order to kill them.

Little D and Geez did not react fast enough as multiple guns fired on them. The loud roaring of the guns going off echoed through the warehouse as the flashes of fire from the weapons brightened each time the triggers were pulled.

Little D and Geez were both on the ground lifeless and dead to the world. Neither of them saw this coming. They figured if they paid the money as Tommy Guns did, they would be able to continue doing business with him. On the other hand, Tony also feared his connect, the bossy voice over the phone that got at him about having problems like this.

Had Tommy Guns known what had just happened to his young bucks, he would set out to kill Tony himself, and all of his goons if he could. The scene was a true Miami massacre. Tony wanted to have Tre there, too, but Tre's instincts made him not show up.

Tony was now focused on cleaning up the mess he had made by investing product and time with Tommy Guns. Everybody must go. He did not want to chance it with him striking a deal with the Feds. Little did Tony know that was not Tommy's style. He would take a bullet to the face first. After his men killed them, they made their way over to the projects to find Tre and take him out.

~ ~ ~

At 10:04 a.m. two H2 Hummers with Tony's men pulled into the projects in search of Tre. They were ready to leave him where he stood, with no chance of retaliating for what they had done to his homies. As soon as the Hummers came to a halt and parked, all of Tre's little homies in the hood popped up with straps ranging from AK-47s to AR-15s to 22mm Uzis. They gunned down all of Tony's men, not even giving them a chance to get out of their trucks. Tre knew these muthafuckas would come if he didn't show up, because Tony was about his business and punctual when it came to time and his money.

When the gunfire came to a halt, close to one thousand rounds had been fired. One of the doors on the H2 opened up only to have a bloody wounded Latino fall out of the truck, spitting out blood from his lungs being punctured. Tre ran over to the nigga with his gun aimed at him.

"Y'all want me dead, huh? I take it my nigqas didn't make it out of that meeting?" Tre asked with murderous eyes blacked by anger.

"They're dead, punta, just like you'll be!" the goon said to

Tre.

"That greedy muthafucka killed my homies?" Tre said while thinking about Little D and Geez. "Now you're going to join them, fool," he said, before firing a round into the goon's face and instantly killing him. Tre then turned around and looked at his homies in the hood. "Get the fiends to get rid of these muthafuckas and burn them in their trucks." They did as the young boss asked them to do.

~ ~ ~

At 11:02 a.m., Agent Johnson called Jack Ross at his home to see if he had come across any information that would help figure out how Rakman had gotten out.

"Jack Ross here. What's going on?" he asked, after seeing the number on the caller ID, so he knew who was calling.

"Sir, this is Johnson. I'm calling to see if you came across data on the escape. The media wants and needs answers."

Jack flashed back to the previous night when he saw Agent O'Neil's brains get blown out on the highway, followed by the call he received after that. What little he knew was sensitive information that needed to get out, but first he would need the names of those involved. How would he get them? He relayed all he was told by Agent O'Neil to Agent Johnson, so he would not be the only one who had this intel just in case something happened to him.

"Sir, I'll get this info to the media immediately to see what they can dig up after they have been made aware of this," Agent Johnson said.

"Agent Johnson, this may be the last time you'll hear from me, if you know what I mean. So make sure you don't waste any time getting this to the media," Ross said, feeling as if the world he knew was coming to an end, just as Agent O'Neil had met his abrupt demise.

After the call, Jack started getting his things together. He was ready to leave the house and his wife behind. He figured that by making the call, someone may have been listening; and the longer he stayed there at the home, the more chance his wife would have of being physically harmed by the men wanting to conceal the information about Rakman, because it would expose a lot more than just who helped him escape. It would go deeper into those who sided with him and their reasons why. Another reason he wanted to leave before his wife got home from work was that he did not want to be killed in his home and have her walk in on his lifeless body. It would be emotionally and mentally scaring for her forever.

As soon as Jack came to the front door preparing to leave, he was greeted by the mailman. At that very moment, Jack's body seized up in fear as his heart began pumping with even more fear, thinking that his time had come to an end.

"I have some mail for Mr. Ross," the mailman said.

"I'll take it," Jack said, before quickly signing and handing back the clipboard and pen.

"Have a nice day, sir," he said as he walked away.

As soon as the mailman turned his back and walked away, Jack tossed the package into the house and raced over to his car. He was ready to get as far away as he could from his home. He turned the key, only to hear the car sounds as if it was stalling. Another red flag made him think that something was about to happen.

"Get a hold of yourself, Jack. This ain't the movies," he said to himself while trying to start the car again.

He quickly drove off after checking his mirrors and looking around. He then noticed that the mailman did not carry a mailbag, so he looked back at him with a smirk on his face. The mailman was not stopping at any of the other houses. Jack slowed down and wanted to stop, but he did not. Instead, he locked eyes with and tried to remember the face of the mailman, who was looking back at Jack with a sadistic smirk on his face as if he knew something. Maybe he did.

Jack's eyes shifted from the mailman's face to his hands, in which he was holding a box. It was now clear what he had in his hand. It was a detonator that he pressed to set off an explosive attached to the bottom of Jack's car. An abrupt yet violent explosion immediately sounded off, which was backed by fire that engulfed Jack and all of his secrets that he would now take to the other side with him.

CHAPTER 19

BACK IN HARRISBURG, Agent Johnson hung up the phone after making calls to the press, who wanted to get out information to the public. Once he had finished, he made his way to the parking garage that connected to the Federal building. He felt good about what he had accomplished thus far; although he was unaware that Jack Ross had just lost his life over information that would lead to the nation's greatest scandal.

Agent Johnson made it to his car and slid the key into the door. Just as he turned it, he heard a voice from behind him which immediately drew his attention.

"Agent Johnson, sir. Jack Ross is dead. You have the chance to walk away from this alive if you choose to. The moment you stand in front of the media, we view it as a compromise to our nation's security," the militant-looking man in all-black fatigues said.

Agent Johnson knew the trained man would not kill him inside the garage with so many cameras present, so he felt somewhat safe for now.

"Are you kidding me with this national security thing?

Someone is responsible for the breakout of known terrorist Rakman Hussein!" Agent Johnson snapped.

"Sir, lower your tone. We wouldn't want to escalate matters before their time."

"What? What does that mean? What branch of the service are you from? I want to speak to your superiors!" Agent Johnson asked with anger and frustration.

He wanted to know why Rakman was a national treasure all of a sudden, so to speak.

"The group I represent does not exist on paper, so we don't have any titles. Sir, if you stand before the press, tomorrow will not come for you," the man warned as he walked away and disappeared as if he had never existed.

Agent Johnson did not trust anyone now. The fact that they wanted him to be silent made him want to be even more vocal. At the same time, he wanted to make sure Jack or Agent O'Neil did not die in vain.

Agent Johnson made his way over to the Capitol but remained seated in his parked car where the media outlets were setting up to listen to what he had to say regarding Rakman Hussein. He sat in his car and thought of what he was going to do, since he was informed that if he did not remain silent, they would come after him and probably his family.

Meanwhile, over on the other side of the city, Shari and her mother were at her place talking about what they were going to do with the $2 million reward they were splitting for the capture of Tommy Guns. The kids were upstairs playing with new toys that she had bought at Toys "R" Us.

Their conversation was interrupted when the front door was kicked in.

"Oh my God! What's going on!" Shari screamed.

"Jesus, help us!" Shari's mom yelled when she saw two gunmen come through the door with twin silenced 9mm automatics.

The two men were sent by the Mexican cartel run by Hector Guzman, courtesy of Tony the Ghost, since he made them aware of his problem the day of Tommy's arrest.

They did not hesitate. The first burst of rounds from the sicarios slammed into Shari's face silencing her forever as her brains and chunks of her skull sprayed the dining room table before her body hit the ground, robbed of life, because she was no more.

The second assassin fired multiple times into her mom, who screamed until slugs filled her mouth and body. They dropped her where she stood as each bullet sucked the life from her flesh. Just like Tommy Guns had promised, she died a miserable death. Neither of them would have the chance to spend the money, or think about setting up anyone else, for that matter.

The kids upstairs heard their mother's and grandmother's screams and came down the steps undetected, until they spoke after seeing their mother and grandmother lying lifeless in their blood-saturated clothing.

"My daddy, Tommy Guns, is going to get you for that," little Tommy said as he stared down the men, not knowing they came to clean the house of the children as well.

The cartel sicario quickly turned and was ready to take out the kids, too, until his partner stopped him.

"*Oye, que pasol? Jefe dijested mata lo todo cada uno,*" the sicario said.

He wanted to complete the job he had come to do, but the American-born assassin he came with did not want to kill the kids because he personally knew Tommy Guns.

"I can't let you kill the kids. I know their father. He's a friend of mine," Ra Ra said.

"You don't have to let me do anything, cabron. I came here to do a job," the sicario said as he pointed his weapon at the kids.

Ra Ra did not let him get a shot off. He fired multiple rounds from both guns, which killed the Mexican goon where he stood. He then shifted his attention to the kids.

"I'm going to call the police and they're going to take you and your brother away from here, okay?" Ra Ra explained before making the call and leaving the kids alone to wait for the police to arrive.

The police would enter with caution upon seeing the front door had been kicked in. But the kids would be safe and taken to a good place away from this life of murder.

CHAPTER 20

AGENT JOHNSON EXITED his car at 11:45 a.m. and made his way to the top of the Capitol steps, which gave him an overview of the media and people awaiting his comments. All the cameras were tuned in and zoomed on to him as he approached the microphone, ready to deliver the information about Rakman Hussein as well as his encounter with the man in the garage.

Agent Johnson grew nervous when he thought about the threat made on his life as well as Jack Ross no longer being there because of his relaying the message to him. He cleared his throat as he adjusted the microphones in front of him.

"Eh-um, thank you all for coming out on such short notice. I promise to make it worth your while. As you all know, Rakman Hussein's escape was done with precision. I'm here to make you aware of the men behind all of this. The people we trust!" Agent Johnson began, becoming more at ease with his words as they flowed from his mouth.

He wanted to put pressure on those responsible for this.

The reporters' cameras zoomed in on his face while he was speaking. They wanted to capture the words and the emotions behind every word he said.

Then it happened, right before the rolling cameras. A pink mist sprayed the reporters closest to Agent Johnson as a slug from a faraway sniper crashed into his skull, blowing out his brains from the back with force. At the same time, the bullet made the rest of his head disappear as it exploded into small fragments of flesh and skull. His body fell limp and hit the ground, only to twitch a few times before coming to a halt as the shock of the slug sucked the life and soul out of the flesh. He was no more.

The reporters started to scream and duck down when they heard the crack of the gun. Some continued to roll their cameras, even zooming in on the dead body of Agent Johnson. Other reporters directed their cameras to zoom in on the buildings surrounding the Capitol where they believed the shot had come from. But it was to no avail, as the shot fired was from a distance further away than they could ever see coming or going. By the time they figured it out, he would be gone.

All of the reporters gave their views on what had just taken place with Agent Johnson, each of them adding their own conspiracy theory and twist to it. Social media outlets tagged the video, which made it go viral with hashtags with view after view.

~ ~ ~

Meanwhile, over at the Cumberland County Prison in Carlisle, Pennsylvania, Tommy Guns was being called up to the front of the prison for a lawyer visit.

He saw two attorneys when he entered the room, one he recognized and the other carrying a briefcase, who he did not. The other person in the room was Tony the Ghost. Tommy was actually surprised to see him, especially with all that was going on with the Feds. A man of power like Tony must be here for one thing—his money. With his connections and resources, he managed to get fake credentials as a lawyer.

Tony closed the door before getting down to business.

"I never figured our business would end like this. You know why I'm here, amigo," Tony said.

"You came to find out where your product or money is. My crew can handle that for me," he said.

He did not know that outside of Tre, he no longer had a crew, thanks to Tony.

"So where is my product or 1.5, hermano?"

"In a rental storage in Miami."

Tony slid a piece of paper and a pen across the table to Tommy. Tommy then wrote down the address and storage number for him. The key would not be necessary. Tony knew people that would handle this for him.

"Tony, use your position and power to get me out of here!" Tommy Guns said.

"I'll see what I can do. In the meantime, this lawyer is going to help you out with anything you need. He's already paid for," Tony said, standing up to shake Tommy's hand. "Everything will be okay. This place doesn't suit you at all," he said before exiting the room.

The lawyer in the room opened up his briefcase to reveal papers he wanted Tommy to look over. The lawyer remained standing and then pulled out one of his pens from his suit pocket. He removed the cap on the pen and exposed a needle that it concealed.

Tommy was still focused on the papers he was given to read, unaware of the needle in the other man's hand, until he felt a pinch in his neck. The fake lawyer held Tommy until he injected the fluid into his neck, which was a mixture of toxins that immediately paralyzed him so he could not resist. He was alert but not for long as his fast-beating heart slowed down. Each beat made it darker and darker, which put fear into Tommy as moments of an end came to him.

The lawyer laid his body on the floor before walking out undetected as if nothing had happened. A group of men waited for the fake lawyer to exit before they, too, vanished down the road together.

CHAPTER 21

A FEW DAYS later, the FBI was looking for the fake lawyer that came to see Tommy Guns. His lifeless body was discovered floating under the City Island Bridge along the Susquehanna River. A slug to the head was the cause of death. Tony the Ghost and his associates clearly were covering all their tracks. The conspiracy was apparent, with the fake lawyer visiting Tommy Guns who was then found floating in the river. This all made the Feds want answers to their list of never-ending questions.

On the other side of the city at Dauphin County Prison, Nino was being released as promised by Rakman for taking care of business for him. All charges against him had been dismissed due to an invalid search warrant. Rakman had his people secure that, along with other evidence that would taint the case and render it unable to prosecute.

One of Rakman's associates came to pick up Nino and take him to the airport, making sure he left the city and never returned.

"You know you can never return to this city under any

condition? This is all a part of the agreement you've made with Rakman," the white businessman said with serious conviction.

"Fuck this city and the government! All this shit is corrupt anyway. They ain't never gotta worry about me coming back to this city."

Once they arrived at the airport, the man handed Nino a gym bag containing $1 million as promised. This would give him the chance to start all over and find his way. Nino took the bag of money and made his way through the airport after securing a ticket. Once he got on the plane, he had time to look inside the bag, which contained the money as well as a note that read:

Thank you for everything, my good friend. I kept my word; now you keep yours. Allah u Akbar! Stay low and change your lifestyle, and your freedom will be appreciated.

Nino smiled upon reading his words, thinking about how this shit was real and how this nigga Rakman kept his word. He blessed him with money and his freedom. Although he didn't care if he ever saw him again, he appreciated what he already had done. Nino sipped his rum and Coke and enjoyed his freedom and newfound fortune as the plane took off toward a new start far away from the corrupt city of Harrisburg.

~ ~ ~

Back in Miami, Tony the Ghost was at his place enjoying his 70-inch flat-screen with surround sound. He was relaxing after the completion of the cleanup and taking care of business that would connect back to him or cause problems in the organization with which he was affiliated. He heard a thump from another room, so he muted the TV, thinking that one of his men had broken one of his very expensive pieces like he did the previous week, and he had to shoot him right where he stood, even though the piece was insured.

"You have to have a better security team than that!" a voice came from behind Tony the Ghost.

Tony's body instantly froze up upon feeling that this was clearly the end. Someone was either trying to take his reign of power or his jefe sent his sicario to take him out and finish up the cleaning process.

"Do you know who I am and what I represent?" Tony snapped, upon seeing the lone individual sweep around the couch he was sitting on with military precision and aim his gun at his face. "How the fuck did you get in here?"

"That should be the least of your worries. 'Why am I here?' is the question you should have started off with!"

"Who are you?" he asked, wondering if he was a gang member.

"I'm a friend of someone you should not have fucked with!"

Upon hearing those words flow from his mouth, the twin Latinas that were out by the pool came through the door and fired off shots toward the assassin. He evaded the oncoming slugs and dropped low, only to fire on Tony the Ghost. He hit him in the stomach, which caused him intense pain as the hot slug burned his flesh.

"*Ahi cono!*" Tony let out upon feeling the pain.

The shooter now focused back on the two pretty bitches trying to close in on him from different angles. He pulled out his other silenced 9mm automatic and jumped up. With both guns, he took aim at the model-like bitches strapped with multiple rounds and unleashed back-to-back shots that thrust both of the sexy Latinas backward, forcing them to drop their weapons in pain and fear from being hit again. They never thought that this day would come. They figured looking good with the guns was a plus, and most feared Tony enough for this not to happen.

"What a waste of beauty," the assassin said after firing a slug into the face of each one to make sure they would not have a chance to get up.

He then immediately turned around and saw that Tony was gone, but where?

He moved quickly and followed the trail of blood that led toward the front door.

"Your time has come, amigo. There is nowhere to run or hide," the shooter said as he made his way over to the crawling Tony. "Just so you know, jefe sent me to clean up all of the mess you have made. As for Tommy Guns, he's part of the reason I'm in the position I am today. So, like I said, you fucked with the wrong person!" Ra Ra said before squeezing off two rounds into Tony's face and canceling his affiliation with Hector Guzman.

He stepped over his body and then walked out of the mansion, securing his weapons and making his escape. He left Tony's mansion looking like a true gangland massacre.

CHAPTER 22

A FEW MONTHS later, Rakman Hussein, a few American governors and senators, and the directors from the CIA, NSA, and CTD were all in Juarez, Mexico at Hector Guzman's compound. It boasted a 20,000-square-foot mansion, two 5,000-square-foot guest houses to the left and right of the main house, an indoor and outdoor pool, a basketball court, tennis court, sand volleyball court, shooting range, and backyard kitchen for his chef to prepare all outdoor meals and keep food fresh and all of the drinks and beers cold.

Hector also made sure that his powerful political guests were in the company of the finest women in Mexico, who would cater to their every need. The men discussed business, drug shipments, money, and acts of terror to spike the prices of oil sales from which they all benefited. They were all living the life and having everything they could ever need, want, or wish for.

"I like the way our special-ops guys handled that situation with getting you out, Rakman," the Florida governor said.

"It was tragic for Agents Johnson and Ross trying to expose

what we had as well as Rakman," the DO of the CIA said.

The DO from the CTD chimed in with his thoughts as well: "If it wasn't for Agent O'Neil wanting to be the American hero, our guys wouldn't have had to take them out as they did with trained precision."

As they continued talking about business and how life was going so well, more people entered the home. The staff walked over to Hector to get his attention.

"Señor Guzman, you have more guests."

"*Quien es ese?*"

"*Tu familia y ella's novio.*"

"Let 'em in."

Ra Ra and Carmen entered with smiles on their faces as they greeted Hector with love and respect. They were then introduced before sitting poolside with all the women and political figures including Rakman. Ra Ra saw that he was taking it all in, not allowing it to shock or surprise him. He knew what types of people he was around now. This was a league of distinguished gentlemen in power.

"There are a lot of people here, papi," Carmen said, never seeing her uncle's place with so many people outside of family.

"People that shouldn't be here, but they are," he responded as the staff came up and handed him a gin and juice as he had requested.

Carmen got a piña colada, which was a drink that always reminded her of the first time she met Ra Ra. That's what he was drinking, and he shared it with her since she never had one before.

Ra Ra and Carmen sat back down and enjoyed the good life while they observed all of the power that surrounded them. At the same time, they realized how corrupt America really was, especially with all of the drugs and drug busts as well as terrorists and terrorism. It was all a part of a scheme that allowed these men to become rich and even more powerful.

"Carmen, *mi amor*, I'm glad I met you when I did. My eyes have been open to a lot more. As for my heart, that's open to you too," Ra Ra said while gazing into her eyes, which made her smile inside and out.

"I love you too, papi. I love that we have so much going on for us and an even more promising future ahead of us," she said before leaning over to kiss his lips.

As they pulled away from their kiss, Hector made eye

contact with Ra Ra and nodded his head with his shot glass of tequila in his hand. Ra Ra did the same while drinking the gin and juice. At the same time, he thought back to the first time he met her uncle, who threatened him to treat his niece right. He would never mess up with her or Hector. The end of their relationship would more than likely be the end of his life. He did not see being apart from her in his future, so he was secured from both sides of life and love.

CHAPTER 23

SIX MONTHS HAD passed since the murders of Jack Ross, CIA Operative O'Neil, and FBI Agent Johnson. Now the pressure was on the bureau as well as the American government to provide the media and public with answers to the deaths of such public figures, especially Agent Johnson, who was brutally murdered on live television as millions watched and tens of millions viewed it online. Questions were asked; however, no one had any answers.

Agent Miles of the Harrisburg FBI office came forward to speak with new FBI director Mike Davenport. Agent Miles was also one of the field agents who was shot by tranquilizer dart during the Rakman Hussein escape, so it was personal for him to find answers to America's questions.

Agent Miles and Mike Davenport met in Baltimore at the harbor. Both men felt the situation was sensitive, so all information needed to be discussed face-to-face, not over the phone.

Agent Miles was African-American and born and raised in the corrupt city of Harrisburg. He was only thirty-two years old, but the five foot eleven, two-hundred-pound muscular agent looked younger due to good genes, diet, and exercise.

Agent Miles was driven to get all the answers and the pieces to the puzzle that had kept him up late many nights. Having been an agent for the last seven years, he was always by the book and would follow every trail that would lead to Rakman himself. Because just like Mike Davenport, he knew this cover-up was bigger than the bureau. He was not about to allow these deaths go on without finding the individuals responsible or leave any questions unanswered.

The agents met at the Hooters inside of the harbor plaza. They each sat back and dined as their intense conversation of what had been going on continued.

"Miles, you believe with our men being onto something that it cost them their lives? All the calls made to their phones have been checked out, which means we need to find something that won't send us in circles. Whoever these people were that killed these men, they know what they're doing."

"It's not just men that were killed; it's how they took out sixteen agents with tranquilizer darts, including myself. It was all tactical, precise, and well executed. Our agencies have to know who is responsible for this. More importantly, why cover up a notable terrorist being assisted in his escape?" Agent Miles said before flashing back to that very moment when it all happened so fast. "The equipment they used hasn't even come to market. It's only been tested with our military."

"Are you sure about this, because terrorists are known to get ahold of these on the black market."

"Sir, if it were terrorists I wouldn't be here now. Whoever did this has high-level government clearance and is trained on the level of Navy SEALs, Green Berets, Black Ops, and/or whatever else we have that is higher than us."

As the men continued their conversation while enjoying their fresh crab legs, wings, and lemonade, they looked around to make sure they were not being watched or followed.

Director Davenport was a white male who stood six foot tall. He had a slim build, blue eyes, and a close military-style black haircut. He had been with the bureau for eighteen years now. He was forty-seven years old, and he had seen a lot in his years with the Feds, but this case took the cake. Mike was a California native who came to the East Coast for the position, so he was not about to let other agents' deaths go unanswered.

"Agent Miles, I did a little research myself on this thing. Agent O'Neil called Ross on his cell phone, and then the sniper took care of him. Ross knew enough to get himself killed, because he received a call twenty minutes after O'Neil's call. That call could not be identified. The next call made was Johnson reaching out to Ross at his home. That called lasted five minutes. It was also the last call we know Ross made before his demise. Johnson's last call was to the media, and the outcome, as we know, was murder that silenced them all. That is one thing the government and other agencies seem to be hushed about."

Agent Miles got Davenport's attention to stop speaking as the waitress walked up with her perky, full 36C breasts, long blonde hair, and sparkling baby-blue eyes. She had a beautiful smile and Baltimore accent.

"Excuse me, Agents Miles and Davenport, these drinks are from the gentleman over there," she said as she pointed toward the booth where the man was once sitting watching their every move.

When they looked over toward the area, there was no one there. This heightened their sense of awareness and made the two of them become even more paranoid.

"How did you know our names?" Agent Miles questioned.

"The gentleman that bought you guys these drinks told me.

I'm sorry to bother you."

"Don't be sorry. It's not you," Davenport said before looking around and realizing that they had been followed. "Agent Miles, we're done here!"

They both stood up and rushed out of the restaurant to see if anyone else was looking out of place or trying to blend in. They then went back into the Hooters and demanded to see their camera footage to have a look at the man following them.

"They must think we're closing in on them by having us followed," Agent Miles said. "Now if we can get the camera's video feed, we'll know who's following us," he finished as the manager came out empty-handed.

"Sorry, gentlemen, something bizarre has happened to our equipment. It's down. It's almost as if someone hacked into our feed or something and shut it down," the manager explained.

Both of the agents knew this was deeper than hacked cameras. The men behind this who were following them wanted to know what they now knew, and no doubt they would do anything to keep it a secret.

CHAPTER 24

NINO WAS LIVING the lavish lifestyle and lying low in Greensboro, North Carolina, just as he was told to do. He found a line there connected to the streets with its young goons and hustlas in the dirty South. This was all thanks to the money that Rakman had given to him, along with his new connect that he met partying in Los Angeles. His man was a real fly-ass Spanish nigga about his numbers. He also really dug Nino's smooth way of business and being on time with his money.

Nino did what he knew how to do best. He garnered the attention of those who lived like he did but on another level, which allowed him to connect with the people he did. With the money from Rakman and his newfound connect, he grabbed fifty bricks and then flooded Greensboro. He then moved into Charleston, where he allowed the flow of business and money to run smoothly there as well. He was now focused on the rise of his business, not realizing he had broken his promise to Rakman never to hustle and instead stay low. This was far from staying low. He also managed to put a team together to assist him with distribution and locking down all the projects with his pure product from Colombia.

The first nigga he met when he arrived in Greensborough was Dollar, a twenty-one-year-old go-getta and fast talker with a Southern tongue. He was a real hustla from his preteen days. He was all about his business, and he loved gunplay if a problem arose with his paper or in the streets to get respect. He stood five foot ten with an afro hairstyle until he got it braided. He stilled shaped it up with a light mustache. His one gold tooth also stood out on his medium-built frame.

Dollar's team that helped him move the work included Pistol and L-Geez. They were two thugged-out young niggas chasing paper, plus they were all about putting in that work on the streets if need be.

Pistol was nineteen years old, and although he was the youngest of the crew, he was also the wildest. He earned his nickname because he always stayed strapped and found ways to get his hands on the latest guns. Having a gun gave him power and respect, especially with the streets knowing his rep of shooting a nigga just to get his point across.

His thick eyebrows added to his dark stare, even though he had a baby face. Even his smile, with platinum and diamonds filling his mouth, added to his thugged-out appearance. His braids were freshly done and flowed with his overall look. He stood five foot seven and didn't take any shit for being short. He dared a nigga to think different.

L-Geez was the business thug. He always wore shades to conceal his eyes from those trying to clock what he was watching. He wore a close cut with waves on top and faded on the sides. He flowed with his full beard cut close and groomed with razor perfection. He had a slim build and stood six foot even, but his swagga stood out more than his height. L-Geez also knew that by fucking with his nigga Nino, the team was going to have a bright future.

Nino drove through the Carolina winter in his all-white H2 Hummer tricked out with 26-inch Lexanis and two 13-inch flat-screens in the back that flipped down with the PS4 game console. A 9-inch TV in the dash on satellite gave him the luxury of watching all of the channels he desired. Nino felt himself as a balla from Harrisburg, now that this was his home away from home.

Nino was also in the company of his two red-nosed pit bulls, which made his presence stronger no matter where he went. Niggas in the hoods knew these dogs were bred for fighting and attacking on command. Donte was the grayish-blue pit bull with a killa look, while Vicious was all black with white paws and had a threatening stare and growl. The pit bulls always made people nervous when he came around with them.

Nino pulled up into the hood, parked his truck, and exited the H2, allowing the dogs to jump out with him. Both dogs rushed over to the crew who they already knew, but their presence made them uncomfortable.

"Yo, Nino, I ain't fo' dem dogs like dat, man. They can hurt something," Pistol said.

"You good, boy! They won't hurt anything unless I command them to do so. Anyway, what's good with y'all niggas? Everything flowing around here?"

"Yeah, folk, we fitna to step up our game soon," Dollar responded. "L-Geez and Pistol expanded up north a little with new clientele. I got these niggas from the Burg where you from that be coming down this way grabbing heavy."

The sound of niggas from Harrisburg coming through picking up weight drew Nino's attention.

"Them niggas from the Burg, what's they names?"

"The one said his name was Kaotic da General. He be rapping and shit. The other nigga is Da Broxx. He rapping too. So they getting money from both sides. I got they music too."

Nino recognized the names, but he didn't want to let them know, so he continued on with the conversation.

"So, Dollar, you going have that for me?"

"Yeah, folk, I should have three hundred fo ya in a day or so, plus I'ma come at you with my own paper fo; da double-up."

"That's definitely a good look for you."

Pistol stood with his hand on his gun in his waistline as he was looking back at the pit bulls gritting on him.

"Y'all niggas hungry? I'm about to go grab some fried chicken," Nino said.

"Yeah, we always ready to grub. Ya dogs look hungry, too, man," Pistol said.

"Come with me. We'll go to Church's Chicken," Nino said while laughing at his little homies being scared of his dogs.

They made their way over a few blocks to the chicken spot. Nino left the dogs in the truck while it was still running. He knew niggas ain't stupid enough to fuck with his shit.

He ordered a bucket of chicken for him and his dogs, and then he ordered the homies whatever they wanted before they made their way back outside.

The first thing he noticed as they exited the chicken spot was that his pit bulls had locks on a fiend nigga. They were pulling him from both sides. The fiend was screaming and yelling while he was trying to break free.

"That's the shit I'm talking about. Them muthafucking dogs is hungry."

"Nah, this nigga was trying to get in my truck and steal something. You see how my door is wide the fuck open!"

The crackhead was now screaming louder as he felt his flesh being removed from his body.

"Get these fucking dogs off of me!" the fiend screamed out.

Nino pulled out two pieces of fried chicken before calling out to his dogs.

"Vicious! Donte! Stand guard!"

At the sound of his voice and command, they released their grip on the fiend. Nino tossed the chicken to the dogs, and they jumped on it.

"Good boys! That's what the fuck I'm talking about!" Nino

said as he walked over to the downed fiend who had tried to get into his whip. "Why the fuck your dumb ass try to get into my truck?"

L-Geez yelled out before the fiend was able to respond: "Nino! Somebody's in yo' truck, man."

The crew immediately pulled out their weapons and rushed up on the truck. Their guns were pointed at a nigga trying to hide behind the dark tinted windows.

"Get the fuck out of the truck, nigga!" Pistol snapped, ready to rock the fool.

Nino realized that the fiend was just a distraction. The other nigga was trying to lay on him or rob whatever he had in the trick, but to no avail.

"Yo, this nigga here ain't no fiend! I think he gave that fiend some work to distract the dogs," Pistol said.

Nino came over to the nigga that his crew had hemmed up against the truck.

"What's your name, nigga?"

"Ricky Boy."

"You think I was going to let you rob me, nigga? Or was you trying to steal something out of my shit?" Nino asked as his little homies started patting down the nigga and came across a gun on his waistline.

"Oh, you heavy? This nigga got a tre-pound-seven with them tips up in here. You want to take my folks out, huh?" L-Geez said, taking his gun from him.

"What you want us to do with this nigga, Nino?" Pistol asked, all hyped and ready to put in some work.

Before Nino could respond, the nigga Ricky took off running and fearing the worst was about to happen, especially with the young nigga Pistol ready to pop shells into him.

"Donte! Vicious! Get 'em, boys!" Nino ordered his pits to track down the fleeing stickup kid.

Ricky ran fast but not fast enough to escape the pit bulls that leapt on him like a cheetah attacking its prey in the wild, tearing at his ankles and calves.

Pistol and L-Geez ran behind the dogs and saw how fast they tracked him down. Just like the fiend, Ricky screamed for help upon feeling the dogs tear at his flesh. They crushed the bones in his leg as they shook violently with their locks on him. Feeling the intense pain and his bones being crushed, Ricky blacked out, only to be awakened as the dogs started tugging on his flesh.

"Help me! These dogs are killing me, man!" Ricky pleaded, unable to bear any more pain.

"See, nigga, all you had to do was ask me or one of my homies to put you in the game and we would have, but you chose to be a dumb nigga out here," Pistol said.

He then squeezed the trigger and sent one through his face, taking him away from the pain he was feeling and this world. His brains leapt out the back of his head, soaking into the cold, white snow and giving off steam as the flesh mixed into the melting snow.

Once Pistol put down the nigga, they all ran back to their whips.

Pistol jumped in his Black Lincoln MKZ with chrome flakes in the paint, flowing with the 24-inch chrome Antar rims.

L-Geez raced off in his all-black Range Rover HSE with tinted windows on black 23-inch rims.

Dollar followed behind them in his black pearl G55 AMG Mercedes Benz truck with 26-inch chrome rims and TVs throughout.

Nino made his way back over to the fiend real quick.

"You had a better chance of getting high every day and dying slow, but today you chose to die fast," he said.

Nino fired a shot into the fiend's chest and pierced his heart, killing him instantly as his body flopped from the thunderous slug pounding into his chest and sucking the life from his flesh. Nino did not display any compunction in his actions. He was too far gone for that at this point. He jumped in his truck and took off, leaving the dumb shit on the ground behind him.

CHAPTER 25

DOWN IN MIAMI, Tre was now seventeen years old and a force to be reckoned with in the hood. He blew up from the money and cocaine he was pushing from Tommy Guns. Tre respected OG Tommy Guns to the fullest and got a tattoo on his arm to keep his memory alive and well.

As for his homies from Atlanta, he had T-shirts made up with Little D's and Geez's faces on them to represent their gangsta until the end. Tre also kept in contact with Ra Ra down in Mexico. Ra Ra would call Tre weekly to see how he was doing and to make sure he did not need anything.

Tre and his mom moved out of the projects, but he still had the hood on lockdown with a few stash houses. He copped a crib for a quarter million, and he put it in his mom's name along with the royal–blue, high-gloss 760Li BMW with chrome flakes in the paint that shined even more with the chrome 24s on it. The car pissed off his neighbors, because he was so young to be driving a car that nice. He did not care; he just viewed them as haters. Now the young niggas in the hood looked up to the young boss, with him being in power and running the hood's hustlas, who ranged in age from eleven to seventeen.

Tre drove through the Miami hood on a partly cloudy seventy-five-degree day in the winter. He saw his squad of hustlas, so he blew his horn to get their attention. The 760Li came through gliding with the beats low and TVs on so his little Spanish mami from Puerto Rico could watch her shows. He hit the switch, which rolled the dark tinted windows down and allowed the young squad to see his face.

"What it do, folk? What da hood doing out here?" Tre asked.

"We getting to it around here, just like you would, feel me?" the young buck said while handing Tre two $10,000 blocks of $20s and $50s. Without a doubt, Tre appreciated what his young squad was doing.

"You already got that? That's what I'm talking about. The hood is still doing it out here," Tre said while looking on at the bands of money he handed to his girl in the passenger seat.

"It's all we know. Get money and fuck bitches!"

As he continued talking to his squad, the sexy Latina in the passenger seat was still watching the hood classic *Belly* Part 1 featuring Nas and DMX. Her phone interrupted the movie as she took the call.

"*Hola, que tal?*"

"*Es tambien y tu?*"

"*Bueno*. What you calling for, Letti?"

"Raven, I heard somebody shot Tre's big cousin, Man Man while trying to rob him."

"Who they say did this shit?" Raven asked, ready to put work in for her man.

"That *moreno*, Juice, from the south side."

"*Gracias, chica*. I'll let him know," Raven said before hanging up the phone and turning to Tre to get his attention. "*Papi, esta ahora!* We have to go take care of some family business."

Tre stopped speaking with his team and looked over at Raven. He could tell she was serious.

"What's going on, baby?"

"Somebody shot ya folk Man Man. Some moreno named Juice," Raven responded.

Raven was Tre's main chick and ride-or-die bitch. She was born in San Juan, Puerto Rico, but raised in Miami. She was nineteen years old and stood five foot two. She filled out all her curves and weighed 120 pounds. She had long, silky black hair that she kept braided, which showed her natural beauty. She wore no makeup, yet had smooth skin and glowing green eyes that only added to her beauty for her man and deception if you were on the wrong side. Her full lips were glossy yet soft, and she had a mole over the top left side of her mouth, which added to her sexy, natural look. She definitely was all about her man Tre. He not only gave her what she needed physically and emotionally, but he also came into her life when she did not have anyone to take care of her when she was down. She always remembered that and appreciated him for all he had done for her.

Tre was pissed off after hearing this about his fam. He knew that somebody probably had caught him slipping. His cousin was always on point with shit like this until now. Tre turned to his homies outside of the car.

"Yo, Trigger! Jay! Jump in the back. We got to handle some business."

His homies did not hesitate. They were already strapped as they slid into the back seat. Trigger and Jay were both sixteen years old, and both of them knew Tre for most of their lives, which is why Tre selected them to come along to handle the situation.

Trigger was five eight and built thick. He was a borderline fat boy. He was always eating food, but he was also about the work when it came to popping off at a nigga. He, too, wore braids that he had in for over two weeks while grinding hard in the hood. He was definitely focused on the paper. Trigger was dark skinned with a baby face just like Jay.

Jay had his hair cut close and all the way around, which showed off his premature waves that he was trying to groom in. Jay was the same height as Trigger.

Tre stomped his foot on the gas and made his way over to the other side of the city to track down the nigga that did this to his cousin. He knew where Juice hung out and what he was into, being a stickup kid. But he just happened to fuck with the wrong muthafucka, Tre's cousin, who was also moving his product.

Trigger was in the back seat checking his twin nickel-plated 9mms. He had chambered a round in each of them. Jay also checked his .357 Magnum with the snub nose and hollow-point tips that he just copped from a fiend that came through. Tre kept his MAC-11 tucked to his right as he drove around ready to roil at all times. As for the beautiful Raven, she carried twin nickel-plated .380s with pearl handles. She focused on getting at the nigga Juice.

As he was driving through the hood where Juice was from, Tre spotted his truck parked out front of the Chinese take-out place.

"There's that nigga's truck right there. The Cherokee Laredo," Tre said while driving past the truck.

"It don't look like anybody's up in there either," Trigger exclaimed while checking through the windows.

Tre looked around and saw that he was not standing around, so he must be in the Chinese spot.

"Raven, baby, it's time to work yo magic. If he's up in the Chinese spot, do what you do best. Trig and Jay, make sure she's good, alright?"

"You already know we gonna hold you down," Jay said, all hyped and ready to get it done.

Raven exited the 7 Series looking good as can be in her tight lipstick-red Dolce & Gabbana jeans and white D&G top that pressed against her breasts, showing her perky nipples that would distract many men. Her high heels added to her sexy boss-bitch swagga as she strutted her beauty with the diamond bracelet Tre had bought her as a gift, along with the matching nose ring and earrings to set it off.

As soon as she entered the Chinese spot, she got the attention of Juice and his crew, along with a few others and a female who looked like she went both ways, eyeing her up and down like fresh meat.

"*Ahi costiga me.* You looking good up in them jeans, mami. What's your name?" one of Juice's goons asked, looking in lust while awaiting her answer.

"Are you playing hard to get, mami, or you already have a man?" the other goon said.

She just smiled at them before she looked up at the menu as if to ignore them and wanting to get Juice's attention.

"You sexy, chica, but why you ignore my homies like that?" Juice asked.

Now that she had his attention, she smiled and turned from the menu to look at Juice.

"Papi, if I gave you or your crew the time of day, you wouldn't be able to handle all of this and what I can do with it."

"Oh shit! She's a freak!" Juice said, seeing her twerk her ass to lure him in briefly.

"She's just talking shit, Juice. She ain't fo' real," his homie said.

Juice and his team grabbed their food that was ready on the countertop. His boys walked out while he stayed behind trying to get Raven's number. He was feeling her look and the way she carried herself.

"So what's up, mami? You going to let me get your number or what?" he asked.

Before she could respond, multiple gunshots erupted outside the Chinese spot. Juice quickly turned to exit. He wanted to check on his squad, but Raven reacted just as fast pulling out her twin .380s.

"You make another move and it will be your last, cabron!" Raven said, placing the guns to the back of his head and walking him out of the Chinese place.

"You fuckin' pretty bitch! I can't believe this shit!" he said, feeling the steel pressing against his head.

He knew not to try her after hearing the gunshots. It was all too real with how she played him and his crew.

When they stepped out of the Chinese place, he saw his crew lying on the ground lifeless with blood everywhere. He knew what it was and why they were there. Tre walked up to the nigga that Raven had the guns on.

"You fucked up fo' real, fool! Man Man is my peoples, and the product belongs to me," Tre said, wanting either the product and/or the money, since he could not bring his cousin back to life. "Where's my shit at?"

"Fuck you, little nigga! I ain't giving you shit. You want to kill me, get it done then!"

"Oh, you about that life, huh?" Tre said as he pressed the MAC-11 up against the nigga's stomach.

He fired off a burst of rounds inflicting immense pain on him while dropping him where he stood. Tre stood over him and looked into his eyes. He could see the fear of dying setting in; however, the nigga was still talking shit.

"You still ain't getting your muthafucking money, nigga," he said while spitting out blood.

"Jay! Trigger! Check his truck," Tre said, knowing he would still have some money or something in his whip.

People like him would not leave it at home, since they feared someone would take them under.

Through his pain, Juice gave a brief smirk to Tre, since Tre had figured out to check the truck. Trigger and Jay found two bricks and $20,000 in the truck.

"Tre, we got two of them things and a dub, folk," Jay announced.

"You think shit is funny. Now yo' bitch ass is going to die for this shit. Raven, smoke this nigga!" Tre snapped as he walked away and allowed his girl to put two in his face, slamming his head down on the ground from the brute force of the slugs crashing into his face and taking his life on impact.

They all jumped into the 760Li as Tre mashed the gas and raced off, leaving the bodies to lie until the cops came. As they were driving back to the projects, Tre started giving the crew a breakdown of what he wanted done.

"Jay, I want you and Trigger to take these two bricks, break them down, and flood the hood. Get at me when y'all are done. As for the money, I'ma take it over to my aunt's crib so she can have it for the funeral and his kids."

"Papi, when we're done at you're aunt's place, can we

break the back seat in like you said we was?" Raven asked in a very sexy voice while looking over at him as he drove. He could feel and see her looking at him. "You know I get turned on with this gunplay shit. It's like a dose of adrenaline that runs through my body and makes me want to cum."

"You a freak, mami! That's what you is!" Tre said as he pulled up to the projects and let out his homies.

"I'm only a freak for you, papi, and you know this!" Raven said while caressing his arm.

"Y'all need to get a room or something!" Trigger said as he got out of the car and focused back on getting the money.

"The way she talks, you think we would need a room!" Tre said with a laugh as he leaned over to kiss her soft lips and make her happy as always.

"Mmmh! You know you like when I act like that. It turns you on, too. You want it now?" Raven said, looking into his eyes and kissing him once more.

"Business first, mami! Always business first."

"Let's go take care of what we have to, and then it's back to us."

CHAPTER 26

A FEW DAYS later, Nino flew his squad out to Los Angeles to secure a heavy order of 150 bricks of pure Colombian cocaine. Nino took his crew to a restaurant owned by his connect that served the best authentic Colombian dishes. Nino also brought along close to $2 million dollars in cash that he left outside in the Chrysler 300C rental he got from the airport. He was getting a rush out of his new life and how fast money started to flow in with his new connect. At 12.5 a key, 150 came out to $1,875,000. That's a figure he'd triple if everything played out the way he wanted it to.

Nino and his crew talked business and future plans when the waitress brought their food over: pork chops, yellow rice with black beans, white rice with beans on the side in gravy, fried fish, stewed fish, and more of the Latino soul food. The waitress also leaned over and whispered into Nino's ear to deliver a business message.

"Ramon will be here in five minutes. He knows you're waiting."

Nino nodded to acknowledge her before focusing back on

the good food in front of him.

Ramon was the Spanish nigga who Nino met a few months back when he was partying in LA.

Within minutes, Ramon Perez (a.k.a. Pesadilla, the Nightmare) arrived. He earned his name for the way he chased down people who owed him or had betrayed him. He also became a nightmare for those in his way on his rise to power. The thirty-two-year-old was raised in the streets of New York and LA, but he came up fast and ended up on top.

He stood five foot ten and weighed 190 pounds. He was certainly a force to be reckoned with in the business, especially any time he was near or his name was mentioned. Ramon's dark eyes were backed by his dark stare and thick eyebrows. His black hair was combed back with a little gray patch on the side that was more like a birthmark, which he viewed as wisdom that he was given over everyone else.

Ramon was well groomed and had a tight team of security that ran just as smooth as his legal and illegal businesses.

Six men entered the restaurant and immediately got the attention of Nino and his crew as well as other customers as they all positioned themselves around the inside. Ramon then entered with six more men, which displayed his absolute power and position.

Pistol, Dollar, and L-Geez never saw the nigga Ramon like Nino did, so they were all impressed by his power and presence. Ramon's men gestured to Nino and his crew to stand up so they could be searched. As they were being searched, Pistol thought about how he would normally be strapped if he was back East, but now he was traveling empty-handed.

"Nino, this is business. As you know, I have to do this to secure my best interest, which is me, because I am my strongest asset," Ramon said.

"I ain't tripping. I know you have to make sure everybody is staying honest."

After they were searched, Nino and Ramon embraced and greeted one another. Nino began to introduce his crew, but Ramon stopped him.

"No need, mi amigo. I know who they are already," he said, pointing to the cameras in his restaurant. "Before I came here, I had one of my associates run their names and photos. As I said, I have to protect my best interest: me," he said with a light laugh. Even Nino found himself laughing at how deep Ramon was with his security mindset. "So, Nino, tell me, mi amigo, did you travel this far empty-handed?"

"It would be a waste of your time and mine if I did, Ramon. I have the money outside in the Chrysler parked out front. Yo, Dollar! Go get them two bags of money."

As Dollar headed toward the exit, Ramon nodded his head toward his security at the door.

"*Vamos afuera con el hermano,*" Ramon said, sending one of his bodyguards outside with Dollar.

Once out in front of the restaurant, Dollar and the Spanish nigga Ramon sent out with him secured the money and placed it into one of the three silver bullet-proof H2 Hummers that were parked in front of the Chrysler. They then headed back into the restaurant.

"*Oye, jefe, yo tengo chabo para ti, es en auto,*" the bodyguard said before taking his place back against the door to secure the entrance.

Ramon gave a brief smile of satisfaction upon hearing that the money was all there.

"I like when a man comes to do business with no bullshit attached to it, hermano. Your 150 is paid for, plus I'm fronting you another 150 on top. I hope you can handle this. It will also prevent you from having to come back and forth so frequently. We wouldn't want the wrong people watching you."

"I'll be able to handle this with the team I have right here, plus I'm into expanding up the coast, which will allow me to get rid of all this product in a timely fashion."

"No need to rush, hermano. Let it take its own course of distribution, and the money will flow. Therefore, your longevity in this business will be long."

Nino felt his wisdom while at the same time took heed, because jail was the last place he wanted to be after he caught a break dealing with Rakman.

"I like this crew you have here, Nino. They remind me of some friends I knew back in Spanish Harlem," Ramon said while reaching for his cell phone to make a call to his driver, who had the three hundred kilos he was sending to Nino's place in North Carolina. "Mira, take care of that, and drop it off at the location I gave you."

"*Si viejo*, I'm on my way now," the driver responded, driving across America with over a quarter ton of cocaine.

"Nino, your product will be delivered to your townhouse in

the form of new furniture. The product is packed throughout the living room set."

He was shocked to hear that Ramon knew where he lived. That's what money and power get you in this world.

"One more thing, mi amigo, and I'm quite sure you know this, but if you fuck up my money, I'll be a nightmare to you and anyone connected to you. No one will have a chance to retaliate," Ramon said, giving Nino the dark stare backed by his murderous eyes. He then patted Nino on the shoulder and added, "Call me in a few days to confirm you received the package."

He then walked out the door, leaving Nino and his crew behind to think about their rise to power with this new shipment coming to them and how they would distribute it. Nino and his crew exited fifteen minutes later and headed back to the airport, so they could get back to the East Coast to start networking.

"Nino, what's the lay fo' this situation?" Dollar asked.

"We have two to three days before the product lands. In the meantime, we need to network and put shit on lockdown with the deals taking over all the distribution in the Carolinas, Atlanta, Virginia, and Pennsylvania. It's our time to shine."

"I got the Carolinas," Dollar said.

"I'ma do Georgia and Florida," Pistol said.

"I guess that leaves me with Jersey, Virginia, and Pennsylvania?" L-Geez said.

"I'm glad y'all niggas think big and outside of the box, because we about to get paid for real. We just have to stay focused and be mindful of them Fed boys and rat-ass niggas trying to take us down. So be mindful of who y'all bring into your circle."

"You right about that, Nino, 'cause the snakes are out there doing more hating than a little bit," L-Geez said.

Nino and his team made it back to the East Coast and hit the ground to take care of business networking. Pistol made his way down to Tampa, Florida, for his first stop, where he reached out to a few people. He then hit up Fort Lauderdale and then Miami, where the partying and women were, which meant this was the city of ballas and where they came to play and enjoy their money from the game.

Pistol drove his truck through the land of hurricanes. As usual, he was strapped with the latest SK-8 and Glock 7mm with extended clips. He was always ready for whatever. He also thought about the new expansion while driving from hood to hood exchanging numbers and negotiating deals.

He finally came through one hood looking to be on point in the game. The area was flowing with the heavy traffic of cars, fiends, niggas, and bitches. While some were strapped playing their part, others were stunting. Pistol banged his Alpine system with his 20-inch JBLs in the back. As he came through the hood, he slowed down when he saw a sexy-ass chocolate sista around his age, so he rolled up on her and let down his windows, so the music could get her attention. She turned his way after hearing the clarity of the music. Besides, it was Drake's new shit, so she was all in nodding her head to the music.

"Damn, chocolate girl! I would love for you to melt in my hands and mouth," Pistol said, trying to be funny and charming at the same time.

"You like what you see, huh?" she said while twerking to the music.

"No, I'm loving what I see, shawty."

She started laughing and feeling his swagger. Her smile gravitated just as her chocolate skin looked smooth, flowing over the curves of her tight body. Her hazel brown eyes added to her allure, which gave her the look of a young Naomi Campbell from the hood. Pistol definitely got her attention.

"Come here, shawty, and tell me yo' name."

"Mmmh, he fine," she whispered to herself as she made her way over to him. "My name is Diamond. What's ya name, pretty boy?"

"They call me Pistol, but you can call me whatever you like if you hop in and let me get into your mind," he said, wanting to get in them sexy-ass jeans she was wearing.

"You use that line on all the girls, huh?"

"Just you, because you fine, shawty," he said, giving her a look while visually undressing her.

Diamond saw that Pistol was an out-of-town nigga with real swagga, so she gave him a chance to have some of her time.

"If I get in, will you take me to get something to eat?" she asked, being ghetto as ever while working her beauty to get what she wanted.

"If you let me, I'll feed your mental and emotional appetite, too," he said, continuing on with his smooth words.

His main intention was to make money and getting to know her could lead to that since she was in the hood with all the heavy traffic going on.

Diamond got in the truck and looked him up and down. She also checked out the interior of the truck and appreciated the luxury of the MKZ.

"Take me to Checkers. They got good curly fries," Diamond said, sounding so innocent but far from it.

"I hope ya man don't be tripping on me taking you away from the hood," Pistol said, checking to see if she had a man.

"I don't have a man. If I did, I wouldn't be up in here," she said after flipping his visor down to check her hair and lipstick to make sure her shit was on point.

"So, what you doing out in this hood? Is this where you from?"

"Yeah, born and raised in the projects, but I'm waiting my turn to get up out of here if I get an answer back from this modeling agency," Diamond said, knowing she may have a shot with her natural beauty, dark skin, and five-foot-seven height without heels.

"I can see you making it one day. Then you won't even

remember people like me. I'll be too ghetto, and you'll be too Hollywood like Nicki Minaj and Lil Kim."

"I love the hood, but I can't fulfill my dreams here. I'll never be too Hollywood, pretty boy," Diamond said jokingly while pushing his shoulder.

"Don't make me crash before I feed your body, heart, and mind," he said, still being fly with his wordplay.

He pulled through the Checkers drive-through and placed their orders before he headed back to the projects.

On the way back, he got more information out of her on who she was, where she wanted to be in life, and what she was currently doing. He also let her know who he was, where he was from, and why he was in the city. They exchanged numbers and wanted to see each other after today in a more intimate setting, like a dinner and a movie.

As they pulled back into the hood, Pistol took notice of the tricked-out 760Li BMW. Being a car fanatic, he appreciated the big-boy whip.

"Yo, who dat pushin' the BMW?" Pistol asked after he saw that whoever it was could be a potential customer.

"That's my cousin Tre. He got this hood on lock, so don't

think you can come around here putting in work unless you coming to see me," Diamond said, giving him a salacious look while eating one of her curly fries. "That's him right there," she said while pointing at him.

Tre was carrying a bag of money he just grabbed from his squad. As soon as Tre got to his whip, gunfire sounded off. Niggas from the projects on the other side of the city came to impose their will as if they didn't know this hood was always on point.

Tre opened the door and tossed the money inside of the whip before he pulled out his Glock 40mm. Raven got out of the car just as fast when she heard the gunshots. She was strapped with her twin pistols.

"Let's get these bitch-ass muthafuckas, mami!" Tre said, opening fire and closing in on the niggas from the south side.

Trigger, Jay, and the rest of the squad came out banging and taking out a few of the niggas. Diamond heard and saw the gunfire exchange, and she became afraid that her cousin was going to get hurt.

"Can you please help my cousin?" Diamond asked Pistol in the sweetest tone.

"He looks like he's handling his business to me!" Pistol said.

She didn't like his response and gave him a look. He smirked before exiting his car all strapped up.

"I got this, chocolate girl."

He stepped out with the SK-8 fully automatic ready to go with a fifty-round clip tucked up inside ready for war. Pistol started spraying at the niggas at whom Tre and his homies were shooting. He was not only a gun fanatic, but he also had a naturally accurate shot that most people trained to have. It may have come from all the guns he had fired growing up.

Raven saw the nigga that got out of the MKZ assisting them in the shootout, but she didn't focus too much on that because he was helping them. Raven dropped two niggas back-to-back with stomach and body shots from her twin .380s. She then shifted her attention in the other direction toward voices and approaching gunfire, only to be hit in the leg.

"*Ahi Dios mio, papi!*" she yelled out after feeling the burning of the slug eating at her flesh.

Tre heard his girl scream out and then saw her fall to the ground. He snapped and fired off multiple rounds, dropping the last nigga in sight. He then ran over to him and saw that he was still breathing but wounded.

"Just cause y'all niggas don't see me around here every day, don't mean this ain't still my hood! My niggas is still holding it down!" he snapped after firing a burst of rounds into the nigga's body, which made him flop on the ground as each slug sucked the life from him. Then he turned to his homie Jay and said, "Yo, get the fiends to take care of this shit. The cops ain't going to be here for another ten to fifteen minutes. You know they don't care about us," he added before running over to his girl, Raven. "Can you stand up, mami?"

"Thank you, papi. That punta got me in the leg, and that shit burns like a muthafucka!" she said as he helped her over to the car. "It went straight through my leg, so we still can fuck tonight, papi. I just have to get this shit patched up," she said, trying to be humorous and somewhat serious about the sex part.

"You crazy, baby. Now get into the car so I can see what's up with this nigga over there," Tre said, talking about Pistol. Tre closed the door on the BMW before making his way over to Pistol, who was now standing by his truck. "Yo, nigga, what you doing in my hood?"

Trigger, Jay, and the homies from the hood came up to Tre's side to secure their young OG of the hood.

"Yo, nigga, I asked you what the fuck you're doing in my hood."

Pistol was ice-grilling Tre and his team. He was ready to get it popping with the slugs until Diamond jumped out of the Lincoln MKZ.

"Yo, cuz, I asked him to get out and help you. He's with me," Diamond explained.

"How you know this nigga ain't with them?" Tre asked.

"He's from North Carolina. He came down here on business," Diamond said.

Tre and his team lowered their weapons. They no longer saw or felt a threat.

"Good looking out, folk. Damn fools always coming through like it's sweet out here, but me and my team hold it down. So what brings you to my hood strapped like that?"

"My name is Pistol, by the way, and my name speaks for itself. I stay strapped no matter what hood I'm in. I keep the latest," Pistol said, displaying the SK-8 modified as well as the Glock 7mm on his waistline." As ya cuz said, I'm here on business; and from the looks of the Seven you pushing, you about yo' business, feel me?"

"So, you thinking about coming to my hood to lock down shit or get down with my team?"

"I come to expand your already growing business you have. I'm in the position to make you an offer that will set you up to have a fleet of those 760s for you and your crew. One for each day of the week."

Tre definitely embraced the thought of having a different whip for every day of the week, so he took a step closer to Pistol ready to talk business.

"I'm listening, but I don't hear numbers."

"The numbers depend on the quantity you're working with."

"I do fifteen sometimes twenty squares a week. I got the Miami projects on smash, plus I do close to two in raw powder to them rich folks coming through on vacation and partying, plus them celebrities be loving this shit, too, down here. I'm at eighteen even right now."

"I can change that number for you if you grab twenty or more. I can get you down to fifteen and a half a block."

"That's real love right there, my nigga. But what's the quality of that shit?"

"Between 90 percent and a 110 percent pure, with 90 being the worst. Yet still you can step on it twice and have better product than half the fools out here."

"I don't cut the work. I keep it 100 percent as is to attract the clientele, plus that's how I got my hood on smash."

"All you have to do is let me know when you're ready and how much you need, and we'll go from there, my nigga."

"I can hit you up in a day or so. Diamond, you got his number, right?"

"Yeah, he gave it to me already."

"Send it to my phone. I got to take Raven to the hospital. My nigga, Pistol, I'ma see you around, alright?"

"Say no more, folk. I'm all ready."

Tre ran back over to his whip and jumped in. Raven sat impatient and ready to go.

"About time! I thought you forgot about me, papi!"

"I can never forget you, mami. Business called with that nigga over there. He's about to take my business to another level, plus he's about his business with the guns and shit too.

Now back to pleasure with you. We still going fuck tonight, no excuses," he said, making her smile as he mashed the gas and raced off toward the hospital.

Raven felt good inside. She loved her man even though she was in pain from the gunshot. She was all about him and for him in every way. She was a true ride-or-die chick.

CHAPTER 27

BACK UP IN North Carolina, L-Geez and Dollar were networking. They knew that they, too, needed to move the product coming in, so they secured many promising deals. Their goal was to have the majority of the product sold before it landed. The numbers they were giving were really competitive, allowing them to take over the game.

Nino made his way back to the corrupt city, a place he vowed never to return. It was also the same place that Rakman Hussein had told him never to return. That was the second promise he broke. Nino made his way to South Acres and then the P-funk to secure deals and lock down shit in his hood. He was raised on the south side, so he came back to where he started making money. He was a project nigga, so it was really all he knew.

Nino never had any intentions of returning to the city, but it was the only place he knew where he could easily dump forty kilos, or at least ten on each part of the city and Uptown, P-funk, Hillside, and South Acres. The city could do numbers like this on a weekly basis.

As Nino moved around quietly through the city making money moves, on the other side of the city, Agent Miles sat at his desk going over some mail that was sent to him next-day air from Director Davenport who lived in Baltimore. It was close to his office in Washington, DC.

As he was about to open the package, a call came through on his office phone.

"Agent Miles here, how can I help you?"

"The question you should be asking is how you can help yourself," the anonymous voice said over the phone, almost taunting Agent Miles.

Agent Miles's body tensed up when the caller made such a statement over the phone.

"Who the hell is this?" he asked aggressively.

"Who I am is not the subject. What I can do to you should be your fear."

The office that Agent Miles was in was located on the twentieth floor of the Federal building, so he was not concerned with the empty threat, since he was inside a secured building.

"What is it you want from me?"

"Stop sticking your nose into places they shouldn't be, or

you will end up like your old friends."

"I'm doing this for my country. They need to know, and those agents' families need answers."

"Agent Miles, we're all doing things for our country. However, is what you're doing worth the trouble you're putting yourself into? Our country was built on scandal and deception. If you turn over the wrong stone, you could affect a lot of people."

"What about the dead agents? What about their families? The public humiliation of having Agent Johnson killed on national television? America wants these answers, and I took an oath to give them to them."

"Be wise of your decisions, because it could lead to the death of your pretty little family. Oh, that's a nice photo of your family you have on your desk."

After hearing the anonymous voice's last words, Agent Miles quickly stood up. He wanted to know where the guy was. He had to be close to know what was on his desk.

"Is he in the building?" Agent Miles questioned.

"Calm down, Agent Miles. If I wanted to hurt you, you would be dead already. I'm a skilled and trained assassin. I want you to have a seat and listen to me."

Agent Miles turned around and looked out of the window at the surrounding buildings. Nothing.

"How did you know I was standing up?"

"I have you in my sights."

Agent Miles quickly ducked down as his heart leapt into his throat. He feared the worst would come to him before he was able to expose the truth.

The sniper fired a round into the office from his location. The .50-caliber slug pierced the window and into the photo of his family on the desk.

"Agent Miles, take a look at the photo on your desk. Next time it won't be a picture. It'll be you if you keep digging for information."

The call ended, which left him to his thoughts and the magnitude of the situation. Right then he knew the sniper could have easily taken him out before he even answered the phone. He just wanted to get his attention. The sniper's rifle was the new carbon-compound sniper rifle equipped with Teflon-piercing bullets designed for high altitudes and high-velocity performance.

Agent Miles now feared for his family's life, yet he still wanted to pursue this to get resolve for the agents that had lost their lives trying to expose the situation.

He composed himself before calling Director Davenport to make him aware of what just had taken place.

He ordered twenty-four-hour surveillance on Agent Miles's home.

"Did you get that package I sent to your office?" Mike said.

"Yes, sir, I was getting into it when the call came through."

"Okay, finish reading it. You'll more than likely discover more on this situation, and then we'll talk about this face-to-face."

After the call ended, Miles read over the content sent to him. He stayed an hour over the time he would normally have been at the office, trying to discover more information. He also came up with a new plan instead of meeting with the director, because he did not want to risk being followed like the first time.

Agent Miles left the Federal building and headed uptown toward his old neighborhood. He was going to a local bar that he remembered trying to sneak into with his friends while growing up. He knew he was being watched by a higher government, and if they came into the hood, he would notice them faster. Besides, people like that wouldn't come into a bar like this and blend in. They would stand out all the way.

Agent Miles tucked a typed letter with the government seal on it inside of an envelope.

Once inside the bar, he noticed someone from when he was a child.

"Jason Miles, is that you over there?" the guy sitting in the corner asked when he saw him come through the door.

"Yeah, it's me, Floyd. I've been busy working, so you or the city don't see much of me these days. What are you up to?"

"I'm still in the navy. I'm E7 now."

Agent Miles pulled his old friend to the side. He wanted to discuss more pressing matters with the letter he had brought into the bar.

"Listen, Floyd, I need you to handle something for me."

"What do you need me to do?"

He pulled out the paper that explained to him what it was and the content of it, so he would be careful making the delivery to the news station.

"I can do this for you, Jason, but it's going to cost you a beer."

"I can at least do that for you; in fact, grab two beers on me," he said before placing twenty dollars on the counter.

Floyd drank the beers and then made his way to the news station to deliver the letter. About fifteen minutes later, Agent Miles slipped out of the bar to make his way home to the suburbs outside of the city.

When he pulled up, he saw the agents sitting out in front of his house. He walked over to them when he got out of his car.

"Hey, guys, thank you for doing this. If you're thirsty or hungry, just let me know."

"Your wife fed us already," they responded.

"All right. Take care, and no dosing off out here," he said, trying to be funny while making his way into the house.

As soon as he entered, he was greeted by his beautiful wife and daughter.

"Babe, thanks for feeding the guys."

"This isn't the first time we've been through this. Those men are away from their families, so I figured they would need to be fed instead of eating fast food," his wife said, hoping that another agent's wife would do same for her man if it came to it. "Jason, why are they here now?" she asked.

"Deborah, you know I really can't talk about stuff like this. Something came up at work, so my superiors suggested the surveillance," he responded, not wanting to tell her details to prevent her from being scared.

He also really did not know if his house was being watched or monitored from within.

After he settled in, he sat in the living room while his wife brought a plate into him that she had cooked for dinner. His daughter snuggled beside him and watched the television. He tuned into the news and saw the reporter reveal the information that he gave to his buddy Floyd.

"We now have proof and more evidence to come explaining the deaths of Agents Johnson and Ross and CIA Operative O'Neil. Our sources say that this is a cover-up to protect those involved in the Rakman Hussein escape, the well-known terrorist who seemed to have America's elite officials backing him. I know America wants answers to all of their questions, and we here at News 27 will bring it to you as it unfolds. I thank the people who passed this on to us. I'm Lisa Brokowski here at ABC 27 News. Tune in tonight for more on this unfolding conspiracy and the men behind it."

Agent Miles turned the channel and put on the Cartoon Network so his daughter could watch it.

Meanwhile back over at the ABC 27 News, Lisa Brokowski heard from her boss, who was unaware of the special news delivery.

"What the hell was that about? Who gave you permission to relay sensitive information like that without facts?"

"Sir, I'm doing my job here and relaying the news that people tune in for daily. Besides, what I said is true. Look at this certified letter with the FBI seal."

"Where did you get this from?"

"When I find out who it is, I may let you in, sir. I don't want to spook the person. It's clear this person isn't doing this for a reward. He just wants to be loyal to the American people. You want the same answers as America."

After the conversation ended, she made her way out to her car. As she prepared to step inside, she was approached by a man in all-white fatigues who blended in with the winter snowfall.

"Ms. Brokowski, where did this information come from you just relayed on live TV?"

"A source dropped it off," she responded, not knowing what else to say to the strange man coming toward her.

However, she quickly realized he was not there to rob her.

"I advise you the next time your source gives you something, to dispose of it, because you will be held accountable for your accusations made about Rakman Hussein, the fallen agents, and our government. You wouldn't want to lose your job, life, or pretty family you have waiting on you to come home," he said as he walked away and blended back into the snowy night.

Meanwhile, back on the other side of the city, Agent Miles was in his house snuggling with his wife, after his daughter had fallen asleep on the love seat. Jason and his wife, Deborah, were sharing an intimate moment kissing with passion as he felt the stress of the day lift off him while in the presence of his wife. As they continued becoming closer in passion, the power in the house went out making it dark in the house.

"Oh yeah, baby, the darkness is adding to this sexy moment we're having," Jason chuckled.

"Let's stay focused on this instead of worrying about turning on the power, because I want all of your energy to be used with me," she said while kissing on him and caressing his body with love.

He started laughing at his wife's sense of humor. His laughter halted when he heard movement and then saw a muzzle flashing from a weapon being discharged. Instantly, the flash turned to darkness as he and his family were hit with tranquilizer darts, knocking them unconscious, all done with trained precision and stealth movement.

CHAPTER 28

EARLY THE NEXT morning, the agents outside of Agent Miles's house were also coming around after being hit with tranquilizer darts themselves. Each pulled the darts out that had lodged into their flesh. They immediately reached out to Director Davenport to make him aware of what had taken place. Mike relayed the information from his agents to Tony Ridge, the Director of Homeland Security, since this was clearly a matter of national security. Tony was familiar with the slain agents; however, if another one was killed in the line of duty in regard to this matter, it would be a breach of homeland security. So, he promised that he would get to the bottom of this for Mike Davenport.

~ ~ ~

Meanwhile at a disclosed location, Agent Miles was just coming to after being sent into unconsciousness from the tranquilizer dart. He opened his eyes and looked around. He was on a cold concrete floor in a sealed dark room. He could barely see his hands in front of him. Suddenly an extremely bright fluorescent light turned on that blinded him, especially going from pitch black to sun bright with no shades. He now realized what had taken place; however, his main concern was his wife and daughter. He could deal with whatever they imposed on him.

"Where is my family?" he yelled out while standing in front of the two-way mirror that was built into the wall. He even started banging on the four-inch-thick glass, but to no avail. Those on the other side could not hear him, but they could see him. A voice came over the intercom that got his attention.

"Agent Miles, you don't seem to understand the magnitude of this situation you're putting yourself and your family through. Your arrangement with the reporter was not good. It has caused a chain reaction, so you have a choice to make. You can live and see your family again, but you must resign from the bureau. If you fail to do this today, then you'll never see your family again. We will end your career for you," the voice over the intercom ended, which allowed him to hear his wife speaking to their daughter and assuring her that everything was going to be okay. "She's in another secured room. The choice is yours, Agent Miles."

Before he could respond, he could hear a hissing sound, so

he turned around only to see reddish smoke being pumped into the room. He instantly panicked thinking it was poison.

"Okay! I'll do it! Just don't hurt my family!" he pleaded, feeling helpless.

The gas quickly filled the room and knocked him unconscious again.

~ ~ ~

Meanwhile, in Washington, DC, Tony Ridge met with Mike Davenport outside the Washington Monument to discuss security matters. Tony knew that asking around to agencies would put him in a tight spot, because it would stir up tension between them. At the same time, he did not want men acting rogue against the nation either.

"Mike, you have my word I'll use all of my resources to track down as much information as needed to expose all of this. If anything else comes up with you in the meantime, let me know, and I'll do what I can."

"You'll be the first call I make, Tony. We need to get to the bottom of this."

After the two men finished talking, they parted ways and looked around to make sure they were not being watched or followed. Each knew the seriousness of the situation and how lives could be lost in the blink of an eye.

~ ~ ~

Meanwhile back in Harrisburg, Agent Miles woke up again for the second time that morning. This time he was at home on the couch minus his family. Once he gathered himself, he reached out to Director Davenport to make him aware of what had just taken place.

"Agent Miles, are you and your family okay?"

"I'm okay, but they still have my family. I'll be in the office in a little bit," Agent Miles said, with his voice breaking up. "They got my baby girl, too."

The agent on the other end did not know what to say to Agent Miles, having all of this on his heart and mind with these people taking him and his family. Agent Miles angrily hung up the phone and then looked around the house. He felt as if they were watching him.

"I want my family back!" he yelled out, feeling as if he was losing it.

Agent Miles showed up twenty minutes later at the Federal building looking defeated, and rightfully so. He felt shame as if he was selling out the bureau by quitting his job, and not being able to pursue his passion. He also felt weak that he was unable to protect his family. When he broke the news to his co-workers about him resigning and the reason behind it, they all tried to talk to him out of it, especially after seeing him break down full of emotion.

"They have my family, and I can't do anything about it!" he said, with his voice broken and full of pain.

"We're going to make 'em pay, Jason, and we'll get your family back," the agent in the room said, trying to make him feel better.

The agents that were hit with the tranquilizer darts also felt as if they were to blame that this had happened, because they believed they should have seen the men coming. Little did they know, the elite group of trained men never allowed anyone to see them until it was too late.

CHAPTER 29

IN UPTOWN HARRISBURG, Ms. Anderson was just getting back from dropping off her grandsons at school at 9:17 a.m. when she entered her home singing "Glory." She could feel the spirit of God inside her. But she suddenly halted her stride into the living room when she saw something that took her by surprise.

"Jesus, tell me my eyes aren't playing tricks on me," she said, looking and blinking her eyes before placing her hand over her heart.

"Hi, Mom."

"Tommy, is that really you?"

"Yes, Mom, it's really me. I can explain."

"Well, whose ashes do I have right there?" she asked, pointing to the mantel.

Yes, I'm back, America! You muthafuckas really counted me out. Like a wise man once told me, "The greatest illusion is deception. I fooled the world including you, thanks to some powerful people."

"You probably have a bunch of cigarette ashes."

"Why would these people make me think my only child

was dead and gone?" she asked with a face full of disbelief.

"I wanted to tell you, Mom," he said as he stood up from the couch and walked over to embrace his mother in love. "I love you, Mom," he added before pulling back from the hug. "Legally, I was dead because my heart stopped long enough to be pronounced dead, until they took my body from the prison to a disclosed location. There they injected me with adrenaline and a few shocks from the defibrillator to revive me."

She still couldn't believe it as she squeezed him to see if he was real.

"I can't believe it. God really does work in mysterious ways," she said while looking at her son as if he was a miracle in the flesh.

"How are my boys doing?"

"I just took them to school. They're doing fine. Even better when they see you. I tried explaining to them about you being dead, but they just couldn't accept it or didn't believe it. Now I see why."

"Thank you for everything, Mom. What's going on with my houses?"

"I have the keys, but I haven't been there since Shari and

207

her mother were killed."

"Let me get the keys to that house. I left something behind over there."

Tommy Guns had close to $2 million stashed in that crib. Money he made over the years. Now with him being a free man with fake credentials, the money would allow him to move around with ease.

"Mom, do you want to leave the city and state? I got close to $2 million in cash at the house."

"What are you doing with that much money in cash? You better be glad I didn't sell any of those houses."

"I've been saving it for a long time—for times like now."

"Let me think about it, son. All this stuff is just happening so fast. I need to collect my thoughts and pray on it. First, I'm going to thank God for not taking you away so soon."

"Alright, Mom, just remember not to let anyone know that I'm alive. I'll stay in contact and send you money for you and the kids."

He gave her another hug and allowed her to really see that he was alive.

"Tommy, please stay out of trouble, Son."

"I will, Mom."

He hopped into his old laying-low Chrysler Concord that blended in. He then made his way over to the house to secure his money before leaving the state.

Tommy Guns had an open mind about the drug game now since the people who wanted him alive had bigger plans for him, or at least that was what he was hoping. He just needed to stay low until he got the call from those people. Right now, America thought he was dead, which gave him the greatest freedom of all—not even existing.

To be continued . . .

Part 4 Now Available

Text Good2Go at 31996 to receive new release updates via text message.

To order books, please fill out the order form below:
To order films please go to www.good2gofilms.com

Name: ___ _____

Address:_____

City: _____ State: _____ Zip Code: _____

Phone:_____

Email:_____

Method of Payment: Check   VISA   MASTERCARD

Credit Card#:_ _____

Name as it appears on card: _____

Signature: _____

Item Name	Price	Qty	Amount
48 Hours to Die – Silk White	$14.99		
A Hustler's Dream - Ernest Morris	$14.99		
A Hustler's Dream 2 - Ernest Morris	$14.99		
A Thug's Devotion – J. L. Rose and J. M. McMillon	$14.99		
All Eyes on Tommy Gunz – Warren Holloway	$14.99		
All Eyes on Tommy Gunz 2 – Warren Holloway	$14.99		
All Eyes on Tommy Gunz 3 – Warren Holloway	$14.99		
All Eyes on Tommy Gunz 4 – Warren Holloway	$14.99		
Black Reign – Ernest Morris	$14.99		
Bloody Mayhem Down South – Trayvon Jackson	$14.99		
Bloody Mayhem Down South 2 – Trayvon Jackson	$14.99		
Business Is Business – Silk White	$14.99		
Business Is Business 2 – Silk White	$14.99		
Business Is Business 3 – Silk White	$14.99		
Childhood Sweethearts – Jacob Spears	$14.99		
Childhood Sweethearts 2 – Jacob Spears	$14.99		
Childhood Sweethearts 3 - Jacob Spears	$14.99		
Childhood Sweethearts 4 - Jacob Spears	$14.99		
Connected To The Plug – Dwan Marquis Williams	$14.99		
Connected To The Plug 2 – Dwan Marquis Williams	$14.99		
Connected To The Plug 3 – Dwan Williams	$14.99		
Deadly Reunion – Ernest Morris	$14.99		
Dream's Life – Assa Raymond Baker	$14.99		
Flipping Numbers – Ernest Morris	$14.99		
Flipping Numbers 2 – Ernest Morris	$14.99		
He Loves Me, He Loves You Not - Mychea	$14.99		

He Loves Me, He Loves You Not 2 - Mychea	$14.99		
He Loves Me, He Loves You Not 3 - Mychea	$14.99		
He Loves Me, He Loves You Not 4 – Mychea	$14.99		
He Loves Me, He Loves You Not 5 – Mychea	$14.99		
Lord of My Land – Jay Morrison	$14.99		
Lost and Turned Out – Ernest Morris	$14.99		
Love Hates Violence – De'Wayne Maris	$14.99		
Married To Da Streets – Silk White	$14.99		
M.E.R.C. - Make Every Rep Count Health and Fitness	$14.99		
Money Make Me Cum – Ernest Morris	$14.99		
My Besties – Asia Hill	$14.99		
My Besties 2 – Asia Hill	$14.99		
My Besties 3 – Asia Hill	$14.99		
My Besties 4 – Asia Hill	$14.99		
My Boyfriend's Wife - Mychea	$14.99		
My Boyfriend's Wife 2 – Mychea	$14.99		
My Brothers Envy – J. L. Rose	$14.99		
My Brothers Envy 2 – J. L. Rose	$14.99		
Naughty Housewives – Ernest Morris	$14.99		
Naughty Housewives 2 – Ernest Morris	$14.99		
Naughty Housewives 3 – Ernest Morris	$14.99		
Naughty Housewives 4 – Ernest Morris	$14.99		
Never Be The Same – Silk White	$14.99		
Shades of Revenge – Assa Raymond Baker	$14.99		
Slumped – Jason Brent	$14.99		
Someone's Gonna Get It – Mychea	$14.99		
Stranded – Silk White	$14.99		
Supreme & Justice – Ernest Morris	$14.99		
Supreme & Justice 2 – Ernest Morris	$14.99		
Supreme & Justice 3 – Ernest Morris	$14.99		
Tears of a Hustler - Silk White	$14.99		
Tears of a Hustler 2 - Silk White	$14.99		
Tears of a Hustler 3 - Silk White	$14.99		

Tears of a Hustler 4- Silk White	$14.99		
Tears of a Hustler 5 – Silk White	$14.99		
Tears of a Hustler 6 – Silk White	$14.99		
The Panty Ripper - Reality Way	$14.99		
The Panty Ripper 3 – Reality Way	$14.99		
The Solution – Jay Morrison	$14.99		
The Teflon Queen – Silk White	$14.99		
The Teflon Queen 2 – Silk White	$14.99		
The Teflon Queen 3 – Silk White	$14.99		
The Teflon Queen 4 – Silk White	$14.99		
The Teflon Queen 5 – Silk White	$14.99		
The Teflon Queen 6 - Silk White	$14.99		
The Vacation – Silk White	$14.99		
Tied To A Boss - J.L. Rose	$14.99		
Tied To A Boss 2 - J.L. Rose	$14.99		
Tied To A Boss 3 - J.L. Rose	$14.99		
Tied To A Boss 4 - J.L. Rose	$14.99		
Tied To A Boss 5 - J.L. Rose	$14.99		
Time Is Money - Silk White	$14.99		
Tomorrow's Not Promised – Robert Torres	$14.99		
Tomorrow's Not Promised 2 – Robert Torres	$14.99		
Two Mask One Heart – Jacob Spears and Trayvon Jackson	$14.99		
Two Mask One Heart 2 – Jacob Spears and Trayvon Jackson	$14.99		
Two Mask One Heart 3 – Jacob Spears and Trayvon Jackson	$14.99		
Wrong Place Wrong Time – Silk White	$14.99		
Young Goonz – Reality Way	$14.99		
Subtotal:			
Tax:			
Shipping (Free) U.S. Media Mail:			
Total:			

Make Checks Payable To:
Good2Go Publishing
7311 W Glass Lane,
Laveen, AZ 85339

an be obtained
.com
A
121218
LV00023B/306/P